Air

Also by John Boyne

Air

JOHN BOYNE

doubleday

TRANSWORLD PUBLISHERS
Penguin Random House, One Embassy Gardens,
8 Viaduct Gardens, London SW11 7BW
www.penguin.co.uk

Transworld is part of the Penguin Random House group of companies
whose addresses can be found at global.penguinrandomhouse.com

Penguin
Random House
UK

First published in Great Britain in 2025 by Doubleday
an imprint of Transworld Publishers

A CIP catalogue record for this book
is available from the British Library.

ISBN 9780857529855

Typeset in 11/14.5pt Dante MT Std by Jouve (UK), Milton Keynes
Printed and bound in Great Britain by Clays Ltd, Elcograf S.p.A.

The authorized representative in the EEA is Penguin Random House Ireland,
Morrison Chambers, 32 Nassau Street, Dublin D02 YH68.

Penguin Random House is committed to a sustainable future
for our business, our readers and our planet. This book is made
from Forest Stewardship Council® certified paper.

I

IN AN IDEAL WORLD, I would be spending my fortieth birthday in a bar overlooking Bondi Beach, a beer in my left hand, a woman I love by my right, while friends tease me about my receding hairline. Instead, I'm standing near Gate 10 in Sydney Airport, preparing for twenty hours in the air with only a recalcitrant teenage boy for company. But who among us lives in an ideal world?

Granted, it's early in the morning, but I'm disproportionately irritated when I emerge from the gents to find that Emmet is not seated where I left him, his bright yellow backpack abandoned on a chair next to my own. I look around, my gaze darting between sleepy-eyed passengers, cleaning staff and airline crew, all making their way through the concourse.

It's not the first time I've lost my son. When he was five, I let go of his hand for a moment in David Jones on Castlereagh Street and it was almost thirty minutes before I found him again, sitting in a corner of kitchenware, with the patience of an obedient puppy, his cheeks streaked with tears but hopeful that his master will return for him sooner or later. Most parents are at their most protective when their children are infants, but I'm the opposite, having become increasingly vigilant since he turned fourteen a few months ago. I can't help myself. I know the dangers out there for boys his age.

A woman stops before me, probably noticing the uneasy expression on my face.

'Are you all right?' she asks.

'It's my son,' I tell her. 'I told him to wait for me but—'

'I thought it was something like that. Look, I'm not on duty, I'm catching a flight, but I'm a police officer and can help if you like. When did you last see him?'

'Just a few minutes ago. I went to the bathroom and—'

'How old is he?'

When I tell her, she studies me with a mixture of incredulity and pity.

'Oh, for Christ's sake,' she says. 'I thought you meant a toddler. He'll be around here somewhere. You can't lose teenagers, as much as we might want to sometimes.'

A moment later he appears from behind me. He must have followed me into the bathroom and used one of the cubicles.

'What?' he asks when I glare at him.

'This is him?' the woman asks, and I nod.

'Yes.'

'Then I'll leave you to it,' she says, walking away.

'I didn't know where you were,' I tell him when she's out of earshot.

'I needed to go,' he says slowly, as if speaking to someone of limited intelligence, a tone he's increasingly adopted with me in recent times.

'I asked you to wait with the bags.'

He rolls his eyes. If this gesture was ever to become an Olympic sport, he'd be Australia's number-one hope. 'Can I get some chocolate?' he asks. 'I didn't have any breakfast.'

'You said you weren't hungry.'

'Because you got me out of bed at three in the morning. Of course I wasn't hungry.'

I made sure we had everything packed by yesterday afternoon so there would be nothing for either of us to do but take quick showers when our alarms went off, but the taxi still picked us up from North Bondi at three thirty. Neither of us uttered a word on the way to the airport, Emmet wearing completely superfluous sunglasses along with the AirPods that have become my mortal enemy. But it's important not to get the day off to a bad start. We're going to be in each other's company for an extended period and if we're going to survive this trip without killing each other, then it's down to me, as the adult, to adapt to my son's mood swings.

'An apple might be better,' I suggest, knowing exactly how this will be received. 'Or maybe we could find some ham-and-cheese croissants.'

'Nah. Chocolate. I need some for the plane too.'

'Fine,' I say, leading him towards a Relay, where he loses himself before a wall of processed sugar. He's always had a sweet tooth but never seems to put a pound on. If I ate half the trash that he does, they'd have to wheel me home. I watch him from behind, his bare legs bronzed and slender from spending so much time at the beach, and recall when my own body was as slim and athletic as his. I'm still pretty fit, for my age, even if the belt buckle is starting to loosen by a notch. I run and I surf, although Damian – Emmet's closest friend – recently said that what I do isn't surfing at all, it's controlled drowning, which set them both off in near hysterics of laughter. That said, Emmet isn't as tall as I was at that age and, at only five foot seven, remains shorter than most of his friends. Although he'd never articulate it, I suspect he's hoping for a growth spurt soon. He recently bought some dumbbells, trying to add some muscle to his lean frame, and he's started buying enormous tubs of protein powder that he's adding to his morning milkshakes.

I make my way towards the magazines, where I pick up a copy of GQ, a crossword book and the *Sydney Morning Herald*, scanning the headlines quickly. Turning away, my eyes land on a table holding a selection of the latest fiction and, at its centre, is a pile of the new novel by Furia Flyte. A miniature cardboard cut-out of the author is propped up, showing her with her head turned coquettishly to the left, an enigmatic smile on her face. She's dressed entirely in white, which only accentuates the blackness of her skin, and her arms are wrapped around her body. Something in the pose seems a little strained, as if she's uncomfortable connecting her beauty to her work but has been convinced to do so.

'It only happens with women,' she told me once, when I quizzed her about the machinations of the publishing industry.

'Maybe because all the men are ugly,' I suggested, and she shook her head, listing four or five male novelists who she considered handsome, none of whom I had ever heard of but who I looked up online afterwards to see what they wore, how they styled their hair, how they presented themselves to the world, looking for tips as to how to model myself on them so that she might fall for me as I fell for her. Studying their author pictures, and the pained expressions on their faces as they stared into the middle distance, looking for all the world as if someone had asked them to explain Fermat's Last Theorem, they seemed more constipated than anything else.

Being confronted by her image now, however, feels like a punch to the guts, a complicated blend of lingering desire and anger. Since its publication, I've done all I can to avoid Furia's book – her fourth – which hasn't been easy, as it's been heavily promoted. Her picture has appeared on the front page of weekend supplements and, driving into work, I've occasionally been forced to turn off the radio when she's been announced as a guest. I haven't even set foot in a Dymocks store since Christmas for fear of being confronted by it and, while I've never been a big reader, I usually have a thriller on the go. But some masochistic urge forces me to pick it up now and read the blurb on the back. I already know the basic story, which concerns the relationship between an indigenous female drover in nineteenth-century Western Australia, a travelling magician and the magician's wife, and I grit my teeth as I read the synopsis. I can't bring myself to turn to the dedication or acknowledgements pages so return it to the pile. Just as I do, a woman's hand reaches out to lift it.

'You haven't lost him again, I hope?' she asks, and I realize it's the policewoman from earlier.

'No,' I say, nodding across the shop, but Emmet's pulled another disappearing trick, causing me a fresh burst of irritation. 'Oh, for fuck's sake,' I mutter.

'Perhaps you should keep him on a leash.'

'It would make life a lot easier.'

'I'm just teasing,' she says. 'I have one of them at home myself. A teenager, I mean, not a leash. So I know what they're like. Bloody nightmare, most of the time. Sweetest kid on the planet till puberty hit and then, bang, Hannibal Lecter without the charm. I've basically decided to stay out of his way until he turns twenty. Maybe twenty-five.'

Looking around, I discover him standing before a display of neck cushions. He's placed one around his neck and I know that he's going to ask me to buy it for him. Sure enough, he trots my way, holding it out like a peace offering, one that I'm expected to pay for.

'Dad—' he says, but I cut him off. There's no way I'm spending eighty dollars on something so pointless.

'No,' I say.

'But—'

'Emmet, no. There'll be plenty of pillows on the plane. Those things aren't even comfortable. They just look like they are.'

He glances towards the woman and, perhaps because she's present, decides not to make a fuss. He notices the book she's holding, however, and an opportunity for payback presents itself.

'You should buy that,' he tells her. 'It got great reviews. Well researched. Unreliable narrator. Literally *everyone* is reading it.'

'Literally *everyone* isn't,' I say, making inverted comma symbols in the air, but he saunters away without catching my eye, a self-satisfied smirk spreading across his face as he returns the cushion to where he found it.

'He doesn't seem that bad,' she says, turning to me, but I say nothing. It's hard not to admire my son's ability to offer a *fuck you* without actually saying the words.

'No, he's a total charmer,' I reply, laughing a little to myself.

Over the Tannoy, I hear an announcement that our flight will begin boarding shortly and make my way towards the till, paying for more chocolate and gelatinous sweets than any human being should consume in a month.

'And these,' says Emmet, appearing by my side now and throwing in a party-size bag of Honey Soy Chicken crisps, enough to feed a family of four.

'For fuck's sake,' I say. 'You do know there'll be food on the plane, right?'

'It's always smart to bring your own supplies.'

It's simpler just to buy what he wants. After all, I'm tired. I'm anxious. I'm undertaking a journey that might prove to be an enormous mistake. And yet, despite my early-morning crankiness, as we head towards the gate I feel a desperate desire to pull my son into an embrace, to press his body against my own and explain to him how important the next few days will be for both of us. I can't, of course. If I even tried to touch him, he'd push me away in mortification. And this from a boy who once loved nothing more than cuddling up to me while we watched Pixar movies on a Saturday evening; one who would often crawl into my bed in the middle of the night until he was nine or ten, lying in the empty space next to me while he fell back asleep.

The truth is, he wouldn't even be here now if he'd had any choice in the matter, but he's still at an age where I have some semblance of authority over him. He wanted to stay home alone, which was an absolute non-starter, then tried to persuade me to allow him to bunk with Damian while I was gone. Another no.

So he's here. But under sufferance.

One final drama before we board.

A security guard is standing by the seats we were occupying earlier, staring at our backpacks. For all the fuss I created about Emmet remaining with them, they slipped my mind when we went to the store. The guard, who looks as if he should be studying for his HSC, not in full-time employment, turns to me, and my first thought is that I could help him with his acne if he asked. I'm not a dermatologist, I'm a child psychologist, but I remember enough from my days in medical school to know exactly the treatment that would sort his problem out.

'Are these your bags, sir?' he asks.

'Yes,' I say. 'Sorry. I went to the bathroom and then my son wanted something from Relay. I should have thought.'

The boy glances at Emmet.

'Is this your father?' he asks.

'I've never seen this man before in my life,' says Emmet, and I roll my eyes.

'Oh, for Christ's sake,' I say.

'He just came over and started talking to me and—'

'Emmet, shut up.'

The guard looks from one of us to the other. He may be young, but surely he can see the resemblance between us.

'Fine, he's my dad,' says Emmet, chuckling a little, which at least makes me smile. I like to hear him laugh.

'Can I see your passports?' asks the guard, and I take them from my back pocket and hand them across. He takes an eternity to compare the names and photos to us and I'm this close to asking him whether there's a problem, but restrain myself, knowing there are few places in the world worse than an airport to create any sort of row. One false move and that's it, you're not only off the plane, you're on a no-fly list for life.

'You know you shouldn't leave bags alone like this?' he asks eventually. 'They're a security risk.'

'I know,' I say. 'Sorry. I'm barely awake.'

'Do you mind if I take a look inside them?'

He asks the question politely enough and I want to say yes, I do mind actually, but if I do, he'll probably summon a colleague and, before I know it, both Emmet and I will be taken to private rooms to be interviewed separately. Thirty minutes later, our plane will be taxiing down the runway while we're left behind. And we simply cannot miss this flight.

'I don't mind at all,' I say, a fake smile plastered across

my face, and he studies me for a moment before unzipping my rucksack. There's not much in there. My laptop. A print-out of a paper I'm writing for a medical journal. A Lee Child novel. Some breath mints and hand sanitizers. My irritation rises again, however, when he reaches for Emmet's bag. This feels like more of an intrusion – I don't like him invading my son's privacy – but, thankfully, his belongings are even less threatening than my own.

'Just be aware next time,' he says, standing up to his full height now. 'When bags are just slung around the place, they're a security risk.'

'That's what I told my dad,' says Emmet. 'But he never listens.'

'And I'll just check your boarding passes,' he says then, and it takes all my strength not to tell him to go fuck himself, but the first-class passengers are starting to board now so I have no choice but to unlock my phone and open the onscreen wallet.

'Aaron Umber,' he says, reading my name. 'And Emmet Umber,' he adds, swiping across. They're perfectly in order so, somewhat reluctantly, he hands them back. 'Have a safe flight,' he adds in a tone so severe that it comes across more like an order than a pleasantry. As if he'll return to charge us with some crime if we don't.

'Thank you,' I say, making my way towards the boarding gate, where the woman behind the desk is now summoning business-class passengers forward.

'Sir,' says the guard before I can get more than six steps away from him, and I turn around.

'What?' I ask, raising my voice in frustration. Honestly, at this point I've had enough, and my temper is rising. I keep some Valium at home for emergencies and threw a few in my suitcase in case the week ahead proves more difficult than expected. I should have added one in my backpack. 'For heaven's sake, what is it now?'

'Haven't you forgotten something?'

I frown, uncertain what he means, then realize that Emmet has returned to the very seat where I originally left him. He's put his AirPods in again and probably isn't even thinking about the time. I bark his name and he jumps up, obedient for once, and follows me. I feel a sense of relief when both our boarding passes scan at the desk without further incident.

As we make our way along the gangway towards the plane itself, it occurs to me that he hasn't wished me a happy birthday yet.

2

A LTHOUGH EMMET HAS COMMUNICATED through little more than a series of feral grunts since being dragged from his bed this morning, I can tell that he's impressed by the business-class cabin. He's undertaken the Sydney–Dubai return flight annually since Rebecca relocated there a decade ago, but always in Economy. Despite working for the airline, which would have arranged an upgrade for her without any difficulty, she insisted that it was wrong to waste such advantages on a child. Let him wait until he can appreciate it, she said, and it didn't seem to be something worth arguing about, particularly as there was always a steward or stewardess assigned to look after him.

Although he's never refused to go, I've been conscious in recent years that he's grown less enthusiastic about these trips. It won't be long before he snubs them entirely, which will be her problem, not mine. It's not the lengthy flight that bothers him; it's the anger he feels towards his mother, a rage that's been smouldering within him for some time now, probably since puberty hit. It doesn't concern me unduly. After all, it's to my advantage that he shows little interest in the world outside of Sydney, where the beach and our home in North Bondi is central to his sense of well-being.

'Nice, right?' I say as we sit down. The cabin is laid out in a 1-2-1 formation, and I've booked a central pair with a privacy barrier that can be raised between us.

'Pretty cool,' he admits, offering a small concession to the comfort of our surroundings before ruining the moment by glancing to his left, in the direction of an empty single seat. 'Do you think anyone's sitting over there?'

'Why?'

'If no one takes it, could I move?'

I blink, telling myself to take a breath before replying. There are moments when I think there is nothing more difficult in this world than being a parent to a teenage boy.

'But why would you want to?' I ask.

'Because it's better. There's a window.'

'How about just enjoying the seat that I booked?'

'I'm just asking.'

It pisses me off that even here, in such luxurious accommodation, he'd still prefer to move as far away from me as possible. I'm fairly immune to the sense of entitlement that kids his age have but I do feel that the occasional *thanks, Dad* wouldn't kill him.

'I don't think so,' I say. 'These planes are all organized through weight distribution. They don't like it when someone changes seats.'

'You honestly think something terrible is going to

happen because a sixty-five-kilo boy moves across the aisle?'

'Sixty-five kilos?' I ask, trying to suppress a smile. He's fifty-five at most. The look of complete outrage on his face when I say this sends a knife through me and I regret it immediately, recalling his attempts to bulk up his muscle mass. 'It would probably be fine,' I say, hoping to salvage the moment. 'But wait a bit, yeah? They're still boarding. Someone might take it still.'

He nods, accepting this, and we start to settle in, arranging our belongings. I store my backpack, removing my laptop, phone and book, before examining the menu and small bag of cosmetics that awaits every passenger on their chair. Emmet is doing the same, studying the tiny tubes of moisturizer, deodorant, toothpaste and lip balm with care. Along with his attempts to grow stronger, he's become increasingly concerned with his skin in recent months and I've noticed a range of serums and moisturizers making their way along the shelves of his bedroom, a liquid army prepared to repel the advance of pimples, although so far he appears to have been lucky in that his skin remains blemish-free. Next, he picks up the television control and starts scanning through the endless list of films and TV shows on offer, removing a small notebook from his backpack and scribbling down various titles. This is a boy who loves nothing more than a good list, tracking every book he reads, every film or TV show he watches, his daily steps, his weight, even a record of the best waves he catches. Although he's unaware of it, I invaded the privacy of his phone recently and was shocked by what I discovered there – it's one of the things I'm hoping to discuss with him on this trip – but I've never seen inside his laptop and imagine it holds any number of complicated spreadsheets, along with God knows what else. For a time, I wondered whether there was an element of OCD to his relentless list-making, but I think being organized simply calms him, offering him the illusion that he's in control of a life that has, on occasion, been badly disrupted.

'You know there's a shower on this plane, right?' I ask him, and he turns to me with a sceptical expression on his face.

'No way.'

'It's true. Up towards the front. Only for the first-class passengers, but still. Can you imagine? Taking a shower in the air?'

He considers this.

'What if there's, like, turbulence? Wouldn't you get thrown around?'

'Maybe the stewardess would come in and save you.'

Once again, the words are out of my mouth before I can take them back, and I tell myself that I need to think before speaking over the days ahead. It's a crass comment, after all, sexist and outdated, and he blushes at the idea. At home, even on the hottest days, he never takes his T-shirt off any more. And yet, at the beach, he's always in just his swimmers. Perhaps there are different rules of conduct by the water.

'There's a bar too,' I add, pointing towards the rear of

our cabin. 'We have access to that, so we can go down there at some point if you like.'

He thinks for a moment, as if deciding whether there is something he could object to about this, but, finding nothing, says, 'That'd be fun,' and I grasp at this small concession. I'd imagined him placing his headphones on his head and either submerging himself in films or sleeping throughout the thirteen hours that lie ahead of us. It's not that we need to be locked into constant conversation, but it would be nice to feel that we're not completely ignoring each other.

'What's going on here?' he asks. 'Are we rich suddenly?'

'What?'

'I mean, all of this,' he says, looking around. 'How come you're splashing out?'

'We're not *rich* rich,' I tell him. 'But, you know, we're comfortable. And honestly, if we have to spend so long in the air, I thought we might as well do it in style. It's not like you ever ask for anything.'

'I didn't ask for this.'

'No, but I bet you're glad that I did it.'

'Could be worse,' he says, returning to his note-book and scribbling something down before flicking through the monitor again. He stops at a mini-series from a few years back about a young Greek swimmer in Melbourne with aspirations towards the Olympic Games, reads the summary carefully and makes a note of it.

Since childhood, Emmet has been a natural swimmer

and, in more recent years, he's also become a skilled surfer. For a time, Rebecca and I called him the Bish: half boy / half fish. At first, she didn't want him anywhere near the beach, didn't even want him to learn how to swim, but I managed to persuade her that this was not just unreasonable but irresponsible. A child simply cannot grow up in Sydney without spending half their lives running in and out of the waves. She of all people should know the dangers that water holds for the uninitiated. Now Emmet knows the waters of Bondi like the back of his hand, could tell you the different currents you might encounter every few feet from Backpackers' Rip to Buckler Point, and, along with his friends, has walked from Spit Bridge to Manly a dozen or more times, stopping at every beach along the way for a swim.

For a few years, he made vague references towards the Olympics himself, ambition that are, sadly, implausible. He'll never be tall enough, his feet will never be large enough – they remain a stubborn size seven – and he has no more chance of making it to the Games than I have of performing on Broadway. But, to my relief, he hasn't mentioned this in a while, the word 'lifeguard' popping up in his vocabulary more frequently of late, an idea that I'm encouraging. Although cautiously, of course; too much enthusiasm on my part will only turn him against it.

A stewardess appears carrying a tray holding glasses of champagne, water and orange juice. Despite the early hour, I choose the champagne, and she apologizes that, as we're still on terra firma, it can only be Bollinger. Once we take off, she assures me, we'll be switching to Dom Perignon. I try not to laugh and tell her that's fine, I'm happy to slum it in the meantime. On the other side of the aisle, a young man is carrying a second tray and, when Emmet reaches for a glass, the steward glances towards me.

'Just an orange juice,' I tell Emmet, and he does as he's told with one of his trademark sighs. If any of his lists include the multitudinous indignities he has to endure as my son, I'm sure this latest one will make it on to it.

Further down the plane, I notice the door to the cockpit open, and one of the co-pilots emerges, stepping into the toilet cubicle towards the front of the cabin. I recognize him immediately as one of Rebecca's colleagues from when we first moved to Sydney all those years ago, and I retreat into my seat a little. I can't imagine him scanning the cabin when he emerges but, if he does, I don't want him to notice me. Whenever our paths crossed in the past, we always got along perfectly well, but I know that if we catch each other's eye now, he'll feel obliged to come over and say hello, and I'd prefer that he didn't. No one is supposed to know that Emmet and I are here, after all. Thankfully, when he reappears, he makes his way back into the cockpit without so much as a glance in our direction.

The cabin is starting to fill now and a young woman in her early twenties approaches the empty window seat, the one Emmet had ambitions towards. She has the most extraordinary good looks – I'd be willing to bet that she's a model – and appears to be dressed for a fashion shoot rather than a long-haul flight. My first thought is that while we're living it up in Business, she looks aggrieved that she hasn't been upgraded to the private suites of First. A middle-aged man a few seats away jumps up to help her store her hand luggage in the overhead compartment and she thanks him, her oversized sunglasses remaining firmly on her face throughout their interaction. He tries to make small talk, but she dismisses him politely before sitting down and kicking her shoes off. The body-hugging outfit she's wearing is ridiculously short, barely reaching beneath her thighs, and her legs are bare and tanned.

I notice Emmet watching her, and it's not because she's taken the seat he wanted. His tongue is pressed against his upper lip, his eyes are open wide, and I realize in this moment that my son is straight. To date, he's never expressed an interest in either sex to me, but I've always instinctively felt that he might be gay. I was, perhaps, relying on age-old clichés that are probably as insulting as they are redundant, but despite his water-based athleticism, he was always an incredibly sensitive child, eschewing team sports or any games that involved roughness of any sort. Part of a small, tight-knit group of equally delicate boys, he's always seemed happier either in their safe company or on his own, reading books and watching esoteric foreign-language films. His taste in music too has always tended towards sensitive female singer-songwriters or gender-defying young men. It's strange how a simple, unexpected moment can inform a parent about such an important aspect of their child's life, but the fact that he can't keep his eyes off the woman tells me that I've been incorrect in my assumptions. Is it wrong of me to feel a certain relief? Of course, his sexuality wouldn't matter to me in the slightest, but the world, life itself, I think, is difficult enough without adding an unnecessary layer of complexity.

I try to imagine him flirting with a girl and find the idea close to preposterous. There were girls in his friendship group when he was younger, but over the last eighteen months, they seem to have peeled away a little, the business of puberty forcing a temporary division of the sexes. I daresay that many of those I knew as children, the ones who ran in and out of our home barefoot and screaming, will reappear in my life in the fullness of time as girlfriends in a year or so. It will be interesting to see how they've changed and whether one of them will break my son's heart or have her heart broken by him. I think he's incredibly handsome, but then I'm his father, so it's natural that I consider him to be the most beautiful boy in the world. But what if those girls, or others, feel differently? What if his romantic life proves unhappy? The idea of him suffering any sort of pain sends an almost insupportable ache through my body. I want to keep him safe from all of that. In an ideal world, I would keep him young for ever, protecting him from all hurt. In that same world, someone would have done that for me. But my training also teaches me that to wrap him in cotton wool will serve only to stifle him and prevent him from growing into the man that he should become. It's a conundrum for me, one that I am struggling to solve.

The model – assuming she is one – perhaps aware that she's being observed, turns around, removes her sunglasses and fixes her eyes on my son, who turns away quickly, pulling a book from his bag and burying his face within it. He blushes again, a slow surge of scarlet rising from the base of his neck into his cheeks and ears, and he doesn't look left or right in the minutes that follow, ignoring the cabin crew as they collect our empty glasses, not paying attention to the safety demonstration, and keeping his eyes firmly on the page as the plane taxis down the runway to take off.

We have thirteen hours in front of us, after all. And then, after we make our connection, a further seven hours in the air. Then finally, one further journey by train and boat until we reach our destination, where we might be welcomed or rebuffed. There will be plenty of time to talk.

But should I have thought this through more deeply before booking our tickets? Perhaps, but there was so little time to make a decision I could only do what I thought was right. At some point, I'll have to confess to Emmet that the only people who know we are undertaking this journey are he and I.

That we haven't, in fact, been invited.

3

REBECCA AND I MET in the rather unromantic setting of a chain coffee shop in the heart of England
where, due to the lack of available tables, we found
ourselves seated across from each other. I couldn't stop
myself from glancing at her repeatedly, then looking
away before she could notice me and object.

'You keep staring,' she said eventually, barely looking
up from her laptop, and I recognized the slight tinge of
an Irish accent in her voice.

'Sorry,' I replied, blushing a little. There was no
other way to put it, so I decided to go with the truth.
'It's just . . . how shall I put this? You're incredibly
beautiful.'

Her eyes opened wide, perhaps in surprise that I would
say something so unflinchingly intimate, and her hesitation gave me time to make my opening gambit.

'If I can guess your name,' I asked, 'will you let me buy
you a drink?'

She frowned now, cocking her head to one side as if
to decide whether I was a normal person or potentially
deranged.

'We haven't met before, have we?' she asked, and I shook my head. 'But you think you can guess my name.'

'I'm absolutely certain of it.'

'All right, then,' she said, reaching across and offering her hand, which I shook. The skin of her palm was soft, but I could feel slight callouses on her fingertips. I was this close to asking her how long she'd been playing guitar but worried I might start to sound like a would-be Sherlock Holmes. 'Deal. And if you get it wrong, what do I get?'

'The question's irrelevant,' I told her. 'Your name's Rebecca.'

She sat back in her chair and stared at me, then looked down at the table, which held a notebook, a pen and her laptop, but nothing with her name written on it.

'It is,' she agreed.

'So there's a pub I like across the way,' I told her, smiling. 'A deal's a deal, after all. You can't renege.'

Ten minutes later we were seated in a quiet booth with drinks before us.

'So are you some kind of magician?' she asked. 'Like Harry Potter?'

'Harry wasn't a magician,' I said. 'He was a wizard. Totally different career path.'

'Then how—'

'The Wi-Fi wasn't working in the coffee shop,' I explained. 'So I connected to a hotspot on my phone. There were only three others available: *Rebecca's iPhone*, *Matt's iPhone* and *Toby's Android*. And I was pretty sure you weren't Matt or Toby.'

'Clever,' she said. 'I suppose you'd better tell me your name, then.'

'You don't want to guess?'

'You look like a Ryan.'

'Is that a compliment?'

'Ryan Reynolds. Ryan Gosling. Ryan Philippe. I mean, it's hardly an insult. It's not like I called you Donald.'

'Aaron,' I told her, shuddering slightly. 'Aaron Umber.'

We flirted some more and, when the conversation grew more serious, she told me that she was from Dublin, although she hadn't lived there in a few years, while I confessed that I'd never set foot outside my hometown, except for a brief trip to Edinburgh with my parents when I was twelve. She seemed surprised that I was attending medical school in the same city in which I'd grown up.

'I feel safe here,' I explained, a strange admission, considering it was only a few miles from where we were sitting that I'd experienced the trauma that had caused me so much damage. 'And you? What brought you here?'

'Love,' she replied with a shrug. 'I followed a boy. It didn't work out. He's backpacking somewhere around South America now, last I heard. He left, I stayed.'

'Sorry,' I said.

'Don't be. Turns out I feel safe here too.'

'And that's important to you?'

'Oh, it's the most important thing in the world.'

Somehow, within a few days, we were officially dating. The first girlfriend I had ever had. I fell in love quickly, partly because I felt genuinely happy in her company and partly because I was so sexually inexperienced that I didn't know how to control my feelings. At the time, I was on rotation with Dr Freya Petrus in the burns unit of the local hospital, and the pressure of working under her, along with witnessing the trauma of patients who had suffered terrible life-changing injuries, was proving pretty stressful. Rebecca's generally calm nature soothed me.

'Are you a good swimmer?' she asked one evening, a question that seemed curiously random to me.

'I'm a terrible swimmer,' I admitted. 'In pools, I always stay in the shallow end. I need to feel the ground beneath my feet. I've never even been in the sea.'

'I'm glad,' she said.

'Glad that I've never been in the sea?'

'Glad that you're not a swimmer.'

'All right,' I said, uncertain why that might be the case.

Which was when she told me about her father, Brendan. About the things he had done, not to her, but to her sister and to others. About the effect this had had on her life and the troubled relationship she bore with her mother ever since the facts of the case had been revealed.

In turn, I told her about Freya. About what took place when I was fourteen. Naturally, these were emotional conversations, but what we didn't do, and what we should have done, was talk about how both these experiences had affected who we were as a couple, because, from the start, sex was a problem. In our first six months together, we only made love a few times, deferring to chaste hugs, and something – shyness, embarrassment, self-loathing – made us too nervous to discuss the foundations of such inhibition.

During our second year together, we moved to London, where Rebecca continued her training to become a pilot while I qualified as a child psychologist. Conferences and symposia were held regularly around the country, and it was at one of these, in Birmingham, that I found my commitment to her challenged for the first time.

I had gone to a bar with a fellow student, but he'd hooked up with another attendee, leaving me on my own. I had no desire to return to the hotel so remained there, drinking alone. A young woman approached and sat down opposite me, saying that she'd spent the last thirty minutes hoping my name was Justin.

'Why's that?' I asked.

'Because I've been stood up by a guy called Justin,' she explained. 'A Tinder date. So I've been sitting over there feeling sorry for myself and wishing you were him. Actually, you're better-looking anyway.'

I didn't quite know what to say. I wasn't used to compliments.

'Have you been stood up too?' she asked.

'Sort of. I was out with a friend, but he met a girl, so he ditched me.'

'He just left you on your own?'

'I don't mind.'

'Yes, you do. I've been watching you. You look lonely.'

'Well, I'm a solitary person for the most part.'

'Solitary people bring books with them when they go for a drink. You're empty-handed.'

A waitress came over, and this seemed like the moment when we would either say goodbye or decide to have a drink together. She waited expectantly and, torn between reluctance and desire, I asked whether she would like to join me.

Over the next hour she told me stories of her life while asking very little about mine, and I couldn't decide whether this was a relief or simply narcissistic on her part. Her name was Kylie, she said, named for the singer, her parents being obsessive fans who'd met at one of her concerts. She was twenty-four years old and worked as a receptionist at a talent agency that represented well-known actors, writers and musicians. When she told me the names of some of the people who crossed her path on a daily basis, she did so without any sense that she was name-dropping, speaking of them with neither affection nor contempt and sharing no gossipy stories. She didn't want to stay there for ever, she added. She was saving to buy a mobile dog-grooming van in the hope that she would one day own an entire fleet.

'I love dogs,' she told me. 'So much more than I love people.'

'Most people do.'

'I have a five-year plan and—'

A startled expression crossed her face, and she turned her head a little to the right, covering it with her hand.

'What's wrong?' I asked.

'It's him,' she whispered. 'It's Justin.'

I glanced across the room and saw a young man standing there, looking around, clearly searching for someone. He appeared harried and sweaty, as if he'd been running. I didn't have much sympathy for him. He was almost an hour late, after all.

'If you want to go—' I began, but she shook her head. 'I don't,' she said. 'He had his chance. And I'm here with you now.'

I smiled. Talking to a random girl in a pub excited me. Flirting. Seeing where things might go. The manner in which, once in a while, one of us would reach over to touch the other's hand to emphasize a point we were making, leaving it there for a little longer than necessary, skin touching skin.

'Tell me when he's gone,' she said, and I kept an eye on the hapless Justin while trying not to make my interest too obvious. He took his phone from his pocket and started tapping away.

'Quick, put your phone on silent,' I told her, and she did so just before it could ring. She ignored it and, throwing his arms in the air as if none of this was his fault, he gave up and left.

'That'll teach him,' she said, watching as he departed. 'You only get one chance with me.'

'I'll bear that in mind. Me, I'm never late for anything. If I'm not exactly where I'm supposed to be when I'm supposed to be there, then the chances are I'm dead.'

'That's cheerful,' she said, lifting her glass and clinking it against mine.

We spent the next hour chatting about the usual

things – books we'd read, movies we'd watched, places we'd like to visit – and then:

'So you probably have a girlfriend, right?' she asked, and I was uncertain how to respond. Yes, I had a girlfriend. A girlfriend of two years. But a girlfriend who never touched me and who I was afraid to touch. I considered saying that my relationship status was complicated but couldn't bear the sound of the cliché.

'There is someone,' I admitted cautiously. 'But I'm not entirely sure what we are to each other.'

'Do you love her?'

No point in lying.

'I do,' I said. Because I did.

Beneath the table, her leg stretched out, and when her right foot – bare, removed from her high heel – brushed against my calf, I knew that I was powerless. I wanted sex. Not just for the act itself but because I wanted to behave as other men my age behaved. I wanted to feel normal.

We drank some more, then went to another bar. Then to a club, where we danced. I think I surprised her by being quite good at it.

'Not just a pretty face,' I told her when she commented on this, enjoying this different version of Aaron that I was creating for her benefit. A confident Aaron. A desirable Aaron. A sexy Aaron.

We kissed, and during that kiss, the song changed, 'Can't Get You Out of My Head' pounding insistently through the speakers, everyone on the dance floor bursting into a spontaneous 'La La La, La-La-La-La-La'. Kylie pulled away, looking at me in amusement, and asked whether I'd asked the DJ to play it. I insisted that I hadn't, pointing out that I hadn't left her side since we'd arrived. But I had, of course. I'd gone to the bathroom. And I'd requested it on the way back.

We danced some more, kissed some more, and then, at last, I glanced at my watch. Almost 3 a.m. The club would be closing soon.

'It's late,' I said.

'Time for bed.'

I nodded, looking around, uncertain what to do. Having missed out on all the rites of passage that train people how to behave in such moments, I felt absurdly anxious. In life, I was seen as a successful, confident young man. But emotionally, I was still a stunted fourteen-year-old boy.

'You can come home with me if you want,' she said.

An image of Rebecca came into my mind. My feelings for her were deep and true. I loved her, I wanted her, I longed for her. But without sex, what were we to each other, really? And so I gave in. We hailed a taxi. In the back seat, we kissed some more. I was conscious of the driver, who was tactfully ignoring us, probably accustomed to such late-night shenanigans, but didn't like the idea of being observed in such an intimate moment, so I pulled back, preferring to look into her eyes and talk quietly, stroking her cheek with my thumb.

When we reached her flat, my excitement was equalled only by my apprehension. I wrapped my arms around her, enjoying the curve of her back beneath my hands.

I grew excited by the deep sigh that escaped her lips when I placed my fingers beneath her blouse to stroke her skin. It occurred to me that I had never given Rebecca an orgasm and that for so long all of my own had been self-induced. Another thing we had never spoken of. I was so stirred by Kylie's arousal that I needed to pull back for a moment.

'Are you all right?' she asked.

'Fine,' I said. *I'm normal,* I told myself. *I'm normal.*

'You look like a fifteen-year-old who's about to lose his virginity.'

Normal. Normal. Normal.

'Slow down,' she said when I reached for her again. 'Shall we have a drink first? A nightcap?'

'Sure,' I said, a little relieved as she made her way towards the kitchen.

'What would you like? I have wine, beer. I might have some whisky somewhere if—'

'Maybe just a soft drink? I've probably had enough alcohol for one night.'

When she came back, she turned off the main light so only a table lamp illuminated the room with its soft glow. 'Is a Coke OK?'

I nodded and she handed the ice-cold can to me. An image of Rebecca ran through my mind, as did the certainty that if I went through with this, I would surely repeat this behaviour time and again in the future. I would become a man that I didn't want to be. A liar. A cheat. A serial betrayer. But I felt such strong desire that I was lost.

And then I opened the can.

It must have been shaken somewhere along the way because it immediately exploded, Coke drenching my top.

'Oh shit!' she said. 'Sorry!' I put the can down and looked at my shirt, now stained and sticky, pulling it away from my skin.

'I can help you with that,' she whispered, reaching forward to undo the buttons and, in that moment, I was taken back nine years, to Freya's apartment, a wide-eyed schoolboy uncertain what to do as she told me that I couldn't possibly go home with my uniform in such a state. That I should take it off and she'd run it through the washer-dryer for me.

Won't take more than an hour, Aaron. In the meantime, you can jump in the shower.

When her fingers touched me, I reared back, stumbling over the side of an armchair.

'Are you all right?' she asked, surprised by my behaviour.

'I'm fine,' I said, looking around, trying to find the light switch. It was too dark in there. I was frightened. I couldn't breathe. The flat was too small. I needed to get out.

'Where are you going?' she asked as I grabbed my jacket and lurched towards the door. I fumbled with the lock, and she opened it for me, before stepping back in fear. 'I'm sorry,' she said. 'Did I do something to upset you?'

I shook my head, unable to answer, and ran down the staircase, only glancing back to see her face, bewildered and alarmed.

Not normal.

Broken.

Completely broken.

The following year, on a weekend break to Barcelona, Rebecca and I sat outside a bar off the Ramblas and I asked her to marry me. I expected her to say no. In retrospect, I think I wanted to provoke her into breaking up with me, for her to recognize that the three years we'd spent together, those wasted, sexless years, had been a mistake but one that could be set right if we separated now. After all, we were both still young enough to start over. To my surprise, however, she agreed without hesitation, and that was it, we were engaged.

We celebrated for the rest of the weekend. With alcohol. With good food. With walks and sightseeing and selfies. But physically, with nothing more than the occasional chaste kiss.

I had gone to Spain with the deliberate intention of proposing, convincing myself that things would improve after we made this commitment. Perhaps I wanted to lock her down, so she wouldn't leave me and I wouldn't be alone. A half-life was all I merited, I told myself. I didn't deserve what came so easily to other men. Who, after all, would want to touch someone as soiled as me?

It would be quite a few years later before the possibility of something more would present itself and I would become overwhelmed by real desire.

Rebecca and I might have met in the most boring place possible, but when I first laid eyes on Furia Flyte, it was in a much more exotic setting.

4

EMMET HAS COCOONED HIMSELF into his seat, kicked off his trainers, pulled a blanket over his body and is lost inside a subtitled French-language film. I'm not surprised he's chosen this over the multitude of Hollywood movies available on the in-flight entertainment system. From childhood, he's displayed a quietly intellectual bent, with books and cinema proving almost as important to him as swimming. A poster for Visconti's *Death in Venice* hangs on his bedroom wall at home, while his shelves are filled with a mixture of manga and classics. Only last May I found myself walking along Walsh Bay mid-afternoon and spotted him emerging from the one of the pier theatres during the Writers' Festival, carrying several books in his hands. I felt instinctively that I shouldn't call out to him and waited until he'd disappeared out of sight before crossing the road to see whose session he'd attended. It made me wonder how many other things went on in my son's life that I knew nothing about.

Sensing me looking towards his screen now, he glances over and presses the button to raise the privacy barrier between us. I give him the finger and, as he disappears from sight, it's good to hear him laugh aloud.

I eat, enjoy some more champagne – the Dom now, may the gods be praised – and watch a couple of episodes of an American comedy show. Despite the length of the flights, I've been quite looking forward to my enforced absence from the world and even though my chair could not be more comfortable, I decide to stretch my legs and make my way towards the bar area. A few seats are available on the left-hand side, and I settle into one, asking the steward for a beer. When it arrives, I open my laptop; there's a few emails I need to attend to before I can fully put my Sydney life to one side for the week. Most are related to children I work with, follow-ups with clinicians or parents, in one or two cases correspondence with the police or the Children's Court New South Wales, and I compose each one carefully, consulting my notes, then save the document in that child's file before placing the reply in my outbox. The Wi-Fi works fine up here, but I'd prefer to reread them later for clarity's sake and send them en masse a couple of days hence. I'm lost in thought about a ten-year-old boy who's suffering debilitating nightmares and who I've been treating for five months now, when a woman takes the seat next to mine. I'm barely aware of her at first, but when I look up from my screen I realize that she's not a complete stranger.

'You're suspiciously alone,' she says, and I laugh.

'I swear I haven't lost him,' I say, holding up my hands. 'He's up there, watching a movie.'

The steward, who bears an uncanny resemblance to a young Paul Newman, approaches and she orders a glass of champagne, which arrives quickly, half a strawberry floating at the top. Her eyes follow him as he returns behind the bar.

'Working?' she asks when her attention returns to me. I'm no slouch in the looks department, but Cool Hand Luke has me well beaten.

'Just catching up on a few things,' I say, closing my laptop and extending a hand. 'I'm Aaron, by the way. Aaron Umber.'

'Charlotte Billings.'

'I'm sorry about earlier,' I say. 'I might have been a bit snappy in the airport. Early morning and all that.'

'You're fine. And I do understand. I'm about to have seven blissful days away from my son while his father looks after him. A little break from his tantrums is just what I need. How about you? How long are you staying in Dubai?'

I tell her that I'm not, that we have a connecting flight there, and when I reveal the reason for our journey, she says all the right things but asks no further questions.

'You said you're a policewoman?' I ask.

'A detective, actually.'

'Impressive.'

'And you?'

'A psychologist. I work with children.'

'That probably comes in helpful with . . . sorry, what's your son's name?'

'Emmet. We named him for his Aunt Emma.'

'Your sister?'

'His mother's.'

'They must be close.'

I choose not to tell her that not only did my son never meet his aunt, he wasn't even aware of her existence until recently.

'I try to avoid analysing him,' I continue. 'He doesn't like it when I do.'

'Well, at least he's a reader. That speaks well of him.'

I frown. 'How do you know he's a reader?'

'He told me about the Furia Flyte novel, remember?'

'Oh yes.'

'Actually, I've read a couple of chapters since boarding,' she continues. 'He wasn't wrong. It's very well written. And the story's interesting. I've never known much about drovers.'

I nod but remain silent.

'Have you read it?' she asks.

'No,' I say, shaking my head. 'I'm not a big reader, if I'm honest. The occasional thriller if I want a bit of escapism.'

'You should give it a try. There's this interesting detail about how—'

'No spoilers,' I say, feigning a smile and hoping that she'll let the subject drop. The last thing I want to talk about is Furia.

'Fair enough. Still, it's always good to see boys that age reading, isn't it?'

She catches Butch Cassidy's eye and points towards both our glasses, which are almost empty. It's not long before they're refilled. 'Billy – that's my son – he wouldn't know one end of a book from the other. It's all football and cricket with him. And now, of course, girls have entered the equation, so that's made life even more delightful.'

She waves a hand in the air, as if she wishes she could simply magic all her son's interests away and return him to childhood.

'How old is he?' I ask.

'Fifteen.'

'Then it's only natural.'

'Oh God, I know. And it's not as if I wasn't expecting it. I was no saint at that age myself, so it's not like I have a leg to stand on. But things seemed simpler when we were growing up, didn't they? More innocent. On the rare occasions Billy graces me with his company these days, he just sits there tapping away at his phone with an expression on his face that makes me wonder what the hell kind of messages he's getting.'

I understand that concern. It's something I've been dealing with increasingly in recent years with my patients. I've had more than one child sitting in my consulting room, tears rolling down their cheeks as they tell me how they're being excluded from chat groups or private accounts. A single negative emoji placed beneath one girl's beach photo left her so upset that she refused to attend school for a month. A sixteen-year-old boy whose friend request on Instagram had been ignored for two weeks had become withdrawn and sullen. It's a subject that's been preying on my mind lately as it relates to a problematic issue that Emmet and I need to discuss.

Two weeks ago, while we were watching TV together, Emmet stood up to use the bathroom. He left his phone on the sofa next to me and, despite every fibre of my being telling me not to, I lifted it and scanned quickly through his messages. They were mostly indecipherable, written in some form of English that must have made sense to him and his friends but was like Greek to me. I was about to put it back when it occurred to me to check his photos. They were mostly pictures of Bondi Beach, a few of his friend Damian surfing, but as I scrolled further back, I found something that made my stomach sink.

Three semi-naked photos.

None, thankfully, featuring his face, but I knew his torso well enough to recognize that they were of him, the shots starting at his lower lip and ending with a view of his pubic hair. Who were they taken for, I wondered? A girl he was talking to? A boy? Or someone else? An adult who had contacted him through a chatroom or an app, masquerading as a teenager? When I heard the toilet flush, I had no choice but to return the phone to where he'd left it, but those pictures have haunted me ever since and, despite my training, I haven't found a way to talk to him about them. The invasion of his privacy would understandably incense him. So I've been forced to remain silent, even though, every time he lifts his phone in my company, I wonder about the messages he might be sending or receiving.

'Sometimes I think having a daughter would have been easier,' Charlotte continues, and I snap back to the moment. 'But then you're faced with other problems, aren't you? Girls are so much more vulnerable than boys.'

'You think?' I ask, dubious about this.

'Oh, I know,' she replies. 'Remember, I was one once, so I know what it's like. The sheer impossibility of getting through the day without suffering some form of harassment. Seriously, from the age of about twelve. That's when it starts. Then every minute you're out in public, in a bar, wherever, it just goes on and on. I'm forty-two now and I'm still not out the other side of it. Twenty years in the New South Wales Police has given me the skin of a rhino, but it still pisses me off.'

'Things can be difficult for boys too,' I suggest.

'The poor lambs,' she says, unconvinced.

'They can,' I insist.

'Look, I'm sure there are some who face similar difficulties, but I don't think the two can be compared.' She raises her voice at the barman, who jumps slightly – ironically, he's been scrolling on his own phone, which I imagine is against airline policy – and orders two more drinks without asking me.

'I should slow down,' I say. 'I don't want to get dehydrated.'

'Oh, come on,' she replies, placing a hand on mine and squeezing it. 'You're on holiday.'

'Well, I'm not,' I remind her, pulling it away. I hate people touching me without asking. Or huggers. They're the worst.

'Oh yeah. Sorry. I forgot. But still. I hate drinking alone. Actually, who am I kidding, I love drinking alone, but we're, what, thirty-five thousand feet up in the air? Might as well be sociable.'

The steward brings the drinks and, as he puts them

down before us, she gives him an unsettling pat on the thigh. 'Thanks, darl,' she says, and I notice his jaw clench a little as he steps away. He doesn't appreciate her touch either, hasn't asked for it, doesn't want it.

'I mean, if we are, in fact, that high,' she says. 'I don't really know.'

'37,532,' I tell her, and she turns to me in surprise.

'What?'

'We're 37,532 feet in the air. Actually, 37,618 now.'

'How the fuck do you know that?'

I point towards a large television screen on the wall facing the bar and she looks at it. A number in the lower left corner, beneath a map of our flight plan, indicates our height and position. We haven't left Australian airspace yet; it looks like we're somewhere above the Gibson Desert.

'Clever boy,' she says, turning back to me with a smile. 'Anyway, what were we talking about? Oh yeah, you think that life can be just as difficult for boys as girls.'

'I do,' I tell her, choosing my words carefully. 'The thing is, because of my job, I've seen a lot of things that I wish I hadn't.'

'And you think I haven't?'

'No, that's fair. I'm sure you have,' I say, acknowledging this. 'You've probably seen worse.'

'And you've probably ended up dealing with the same kids whose lives have been fucked up by the cunts I arrest.'

She's speaking a little loudly now and an elderly couple on the opposite side of the cabin glances over, offended by her language. I feel judged by them and want to let them know that we're not together, that she's just a stranger who's engaged me in conversation.

'That said,' she continues, 'while teenage boys are just a bunch of horny dickheads, teenage girls can be just as bad. They'll do anything to impress the smug little bastards. And the boys know that, so they take advantage of it. I can't remember how often I made a fool of myself at that age over some guy. He always looked like a soapie, spent every free minute in the water, then just wanted to get into my pants so he could tell his mates all about it. I mean, you know what it was like. You were a teenage boy once. It's not real if they don't get to brag about it. That's one of the reasons social media is so important to them, isn't it? People want to show off. Sportsmen filming their gang rapes on their mobile phones. And Zuckerberg, Musk, all those weird little men who couldn't get girlfriends in college, it's given them a platform. A place they can make it clear how much they fucking hate women. And enable those who hate them even more to become president.'

'Maybe I moved with a different crowd,' I say quietly.

'In Sydney? I doubt it. They're all the same.'

'I didn't grow up in Sydney,' I tell her. 'I only came to Australia when I was in my early twenties.'

'Doesn't matter. Boys are the same all over,' she says, dismissing this. 'I hate to say it, but Billy's just like that too. And he's got his father's looks so he's catnip for the girls. Come on, Aaron, be honest with me. What were you like when you were fifteen? I bet you were a right little run-around.'

'I really wasn't.'

'Then what were you?'

I search for the right word and settle on: 'Isolated.'

'The shy and sensitive type?'

'A late bloomer,' I offer, wishing I could extricate myself from this conversation. 'Girls weren't really on my radar at the time.'

'I bet you were on theirs.'

To my surprise, I feel myself blushing slightly.

'Don't worry,' she says, bumping a shoulder against my own. 'I'm not hitting on you. As it happens, I have a boyfriend. Six years younger than me. Abs of steel. A jawline that could slice cheese. Billy can't stand him, and my ex-husband hates him even more, but that's their problem, not mine.'

'You know, you're quite critical of him,' I tell her.

'Of who? My boyfriend?'

'No. Of your son. Of Billy.'

She rears back a little in the seat and stares at me, clearly surprised by this remark. She looks away, then lifts her glass and drains it, even though it's more than half full. This time, the barman doesn't need to be asked; he's been watching us and comes over with the Dom, keeping a certain distance from her while offering me another beer. I take it but don't open it yet.

'That was a shitty thing to say,' she says when we're alone again. 'Especially from a guy who can't keep track of his own son from one moment to the next. I thought we were just chatting. Kidding around. Comparing war stories.'

'We are,' I reply, wondering whether I have, in fact,

crossed a line. She's getting drunk, but I've been matching her glass for glass, so I'm probably not fully aware of the impact of my words, and the altitude probably doesn't help.

'Like, I love my son.'

'Of course you do.'

'I'm not some sort of psycho.'

'I didn't mean to imply that.'

'Well, it's how it came across.'

'I'm sorry,' I say. 'Honestly, I am. It's just . . . I find that when parents consistently speak about their children in negative ways, it affects them. The kids, I mean. They sense your disapproval. But you're right, I spoke out of turn. I wasn't trying to be rude. Just offering a professional thought. I should probably save it for my consulting room.'

She nods, considering my apology, and I watch as she decides which she'd enjoy more: pursuing an argument or holding on to a drinking companion. In the end, she chooses the latter.

'All right,' she says with a shrug. 'And maybe you're right, I should lighten up about him. I didn't have much experience of parents myself so I can't even blame them. Mine were killed in a plane crash.'

I raise an eyebrow and stare at her.

'It's true,' she says. 'I was just a child at the time. Five years old. They were taking a holiday together to mark their tenth wedding anniversary and left me with my gran in Parramatta. I was only supposed to be staying with her for a week but ended up not moving out till I finished high school.'

'I'm sorry,' I say.

'It's fine. I don't remember them very well and it was so long ago. But for some reason, despite that, I've never felt any fear of planes. If anything, I actually love flying. Maybe I have a death wish. You're the psychologist. Don't you think that's strange?'

'A *child* psychologist,' I say, correcting her.

'Well, I was a child then.'

'But you're an adult now.'

'Do we really change that much?'

'I think so. I feel that whatever happens to us when we're kids lays the foundation for the life we'll come to have. If we have a happy childhood, then we're more likely to become functioning adults. Not in every case, obviously, but it's more probable. And if we have an unhappy one, well, it's the same result. As children, we don't have the emotional resources to deal with trauma. As adults, it becomes a little easier. We've learned coping mechanisms. Did you get help to process your grief at the time?'

'Nope,' she says, shaking her head. 'We just got on with things back then, didn't we?'

'We did,' I agree. 'Unfortunately.'

'Talking about what happened to me, to them, people would have said I should just be pleased that I hadn't been on that plane too. Your boy's lucky. If something shit's going on in his life, at least you have the training to recognize it. With Billy, I worry that it's something that I did. His father and I, well, we didn't have what you might call an amicable parting. We still take chunks out of each other whenever our paths cross and it's been years since we split. Do you and Emmet's mother get along?'

'My contact with my ex-wife is minimal.'

'And her contact with him?'

'Even less.'

'That's unusual.'

I nod.

'Still, he's a good kid, I can tell,' she says, finishing yet another glass and raising her hand for another. 'Trust me, I have a nose for these things. He'll be all right. He's cute too,' she adds, and I feel something like an electric shock reverberate through me.

'I'm sorry?' I say.

'I said he's cute.'

'Who's cute?'

'Your son. He's a good-looking boy.'

'He's fourteen,' I tell her.

'I know he's fourteen,' she says, slurring her words a little now. 'I'm not saying I want to fuck him. I'm just saying he's a looker, that's all. Those eyes! He'll be a heartbreaker, that one.'

She glances at her watch, then realizes how quiet I've grown and frowns.

'What?' she asks. 'Why are you looking at me like that?'

'It was nice meeting you,' I say, standing up and lifting my laptop from the table before starting to make my way towards the aisle.

'What?' she calls after me, raising her voice now, and a couple of people in the seats I pass turn around to see what the commotion is about. 'What the fuck did I say?'

5

I MANAGE SOME SLEEP and, when I open my eyes, the partition between Emmet's seat and my own has been lowered. He's sitting in the lotus position, his screen turned off, reading, but he sets his book aside when he sees that I'm awake. I expect him to raise the barrier again immediately, but no, he must be feeling bored because he gives me a look that says, *talk to me.*

'How long was I out?' I ask.

'About three hours.'

I sit up and stretch my arms. It wasn't a long sleep, but I feel pleasantly refreshed. I wander down to the bathroom, making sure not to catch Charlotte's eye as I pass her seat, clean my teeth, wash my face, and when I return, he's massaging one of the mini tubes of moisturizer into his forehead and cheeks.

'You're gorgeous,' I say.

'Do you know that woman?' he asks.

'What woman?'

'The woman you were sitting with at the bar. You were talking to her in the airport too.'

I didn't realize that he'd seen us and wonder whether

he'd come down to join me, then changed his mind when he found us chatting.

'No, I never met her until this morning,' I tell him. 'We just struck up a conversation, that's all. Why?'

'You're at a very vulnerable age. I don't want anyone taking advantage of you.'

I laugh, as he's simply parroting back to me a line I've said to him several times over the last year. I always enjoy it when he takes the piss out of me. It reminds me that there's still something of the fun-loving kid hidden away beneath the stroppy teen.

'Can we go down there?' he asks.

'Down where?'

'To the bar.'

I'd actually prefer to settle back with a movie now, but since he's actually asking to spend time in my company, I won't pass up the opportunity. We stand and make our way down opposite sides of the aisle, passing passengers snoozing behind their eye masks, and meet up just beyond the galley.

It's quiet now and we don't have to sit side by side at the wall as the table that allows passengers to sit facing each other is unoccupied. Perhaps a shift change has happened because Paul Newman has been replaced by a young woman whose hair is drawn into a complicated arrangement on her head. When we sit, she approaches and asks what she can get us.

I don't feel like another beer, so order a gin and tonic, while Emmet, with supreme confidence, orders a Tiger. There's a moment between the three of us. The stewardess can see that he's young, but he is accompanied by his father so, unlike her colleague at take-off, she chooses not to object. Emmet is deliberately not looking at me and I remain silent until he glances up. We're both smiling.

'One,' I say, pointing a finger at him and laughing. 'Just one, all right?'

I don't know whether drinking with my fourteen-year-old son is the worst thing a father can do or the best. All I'm certain of is that we're thirty thousand feet above the earth, and the normal rules of life need not apply up here.

'It'll knock me out,' he says in his defence.

'You didn't sleep when I did?'

'No, I watched another film.'

'Well, we still have about six hours to go,' I say, glancing at the screen on the wall. 'Even if you only get three or four, it'll be better than nothing. You must be tired.'

'Not really. Maybe. Sort of? I don't know what time my body clock is at.'

'A little sleep would do you good. Otherwise you'll be exhausted for days.'

'I'm used to flying to Dubai.'

The stewardess, whose name tag reads Noémie, returns, carrying a tray with our drinks, bowls of nuts and crisps, and a chocolate muffin in which a single candle has been placed. I stare at it in surprise, then turn to Emmet, who's grinning.

'Happy birthday,' he says.

It takes me a moment to appreciate the significance of this. He obviously organized it with her while I slept, and I'm so moved that I feel tears come to my eyes.

'You thought I'd forgotten, didn't you?'

'I wasn't sure.'

'Obviously, we can't have naked flames on board,' Noémie tells me, 'so it's an LED candle. You blow it and, somehow, it goes out. Don't ask me how. Witchcraft, probably.'

I make a wish, do as instructed, and, sure enough, the flame disappears.

'Thank you,' I say to Emmet as we clink our glasses.

'I'm just glad that you're still mentally competent and can walk unassisted,' he tells me. 'Considering how ancient you are.'

'Forty's not that old!'

'Welcome,' he says, stretching his arms wide and doing a more than decent impression of Richard Attenborough, 'to Jurassic Park!'

This is as happy as I've felt in a long time. As he takes a sip from his beer, which has arrived in a mercifully small glass, his face betrays no aversion, so I assume it's not his first. Of course, he has a life outside of mine. He has friends. Friends I've known since they were in Nippers together. Good kids, for the most part, and whatever mischief they get up to is not something that worries me unduly as they're generally quite responsible. The worst thing they ever do is stay down the beach when the lifeguards have gone home for the night, but they're all experienced swimmers and no one is ever left in the water alone.

'So,' I say, sensing that he's open to a more meaningful conversation than the feral grunting of morning time, 'how are you feeling about all of this?'

'All of what?'

'This,' I say, looking around. 'This trip. Where we're going. What we're doing. Why we're doing it.'

He blows out his lips.

'Let's just say, I've made my peace with it,' he replies, and it's hard not to laugh at his use of such an adult phrase. I try to contrast who I was at fourteen with who he is now. I was happy. I had friends. I had parents who loved me. I was growing interested in girls. I liked soccer. My father and I attended all the home matches of our local football team, only returning our season ticket when two of the players were charged with rape. And then, one day, Freya Petrus came to our school as part of an outreach programme from the local hospital, trying to engage young people with the idea of working towards a career in medicine, and afterwards, when I told her how much she'd inspired me, she took me home with her and my life changed.

Emmet, however, is different. He's not quite as care-free as I was at that age, but perhaps the times don't lend themselves to that. Other than swimming and surfing, he doesn't care about sport. So far, he has shown – at least to me – no interest in girls. And until I saw those photos on his phone, I assumed that he had not, as yet, had any sexual experiences. But there's clearly something going on in his private universe that I don't know about, but that I need to uncover. If I am to discuss it with him, I will have to choose my moment carefully.

'Well, whatever happens,' I tell him, 'I'm glad you came.'

'You didn't give me much choice.'

'You didn't put up too much of a fight.'

'Gets me out of school for a week.'

'True,' I say. 'How is school anyway?'

'What do you want to know?'

'Anything you want to tell me.'

He glances to his right, towards the window that looks out on to the dark night sky, and shrugs.

'It's school,' he says. 'It's fine.'

'Adults usually say that life was so much easier when they were children,' I tell him. 'When we had no responsibilities, no bills to pay, no wives, husbands, kids, all that stuff. I think we forget that it's just as difficult being a teenager as it is being an adult. A different set of difficulties, yes, but they feel as important.'

'Not for you.'

'What do you mean?'

'Well, your childhood was great, wasn't it? I mean, I know Gran and Grandad died young, but you were an adult by then. Your teenage years were OK.'

It's my turn to look away now. I've always known that the day might come when I would talk to him about what happened to me at his age but, for all my training in this area, I've never quite known how to approach it, worried that it might change his view of me in some way.

'I had my issues.'

'Well, my childhood wasn't exactly a Disney movie.'

'I've done my best.'

'I didn't mean you,' he concedes, his tone softening. 'I meant Mum.'

I decided a long time ago that I would never say a negative word about Rebecca in Emmet's presence. Granted, I've never gone out of my way to praise her either, but I knew that it would be a mistake to say or do anything that could be interpreted later as my way of turning him against her. Such behaviour would only rebound on me in the future.

'Your mother loves you,' I tell him.

'My mother could barely pick me out of a line-up.'

'Emmet, you must remember—'

'I don't want to talk about her,' he says, cutting me off, and I decide not to push this topic any further. I'd prefer to return to the more cheerful conversation that we were having earlier.

'A gym,' he continues after a moment.

'What?'

'This plane has a shower, a bar. What it needs is a gym. Thirteen hours? You could get a good work-out in.'

'I guess,' I say.

'Just a small room with some dumbbells and a tread-mill,' he continues. 'That'd be cool.'

'I think people would spend more time at the bar,' I tell him.

He nods, but I'm reminded of how he's been throwing himself into exercising lately, although it doesn't seem to be having much effect on his body, which remains stubbornly slender.

'What I said about the woman you were talking to—' he continues.

'Emmet, I swear I just met her!'

'I know, I know. I was just kidding about that, but, can I ask you something?'

I nod. 'Sure.'

'Like . . .' He hesitates, sounding nervous. 'Why don't you have a girlfriend?'

I'm taken aback by the question. I can't recall him ever asking something so intimate of me.

'Well, it's not as if I wouldn't like one,' I say, weighing each word carefully.

'Then why don't you? Like, you're ancient, but you're not gross or fat or anything. And, as much as it makes me want to throw up, some of my girlfriends think you're not the most repulsive dad out there.'

'Good to know,' I say, laughing a little. 'The truth is, I was never very good at relationships.'

'You found someone to marry you.'

'And look how that turned out.'

'That wasn't your fault.'

'It was as much my fault as your mother's,' I insist. 'Maybe even more.'

'I doubt that.'

'We were too young.'

A strange expression crosses his face.

'What?' I ask.

'It's just . . . I wondered . . .'

'Wondered what?'

'Like, I don't know if you have . . . I mean, sometimes I've wondered whether you might have some secret life going on that I know nothing about. A woman you hook up with.' He hesitates, avoiding my eye. 'Or a guy maybe.'

I sit back in surprise. 'Emmet, I'm not gay,' I tell him.

'Are you sure?'

'Pretty sure, yes.'

'It just seems weird that you never date anyone, that's all.'

'If I was gay, I would tell you I was gay.'

'OK,' he says. 'That's a relief.'

'You're *relieved* that I'm not gay?' I ask, surprised that he would say such a thing. It's out of character for him to express any kind of prejudice.

'No,' he says quickly. 'Not that. I mean I'm relieved you haven't felt you had to lie to me about something like that. Jesus. Come on. What do you think I am?'

He looks genuinely mortified that I could have misinterpreted him, and I hold a hand up to acknowledge this. After all, Damian came out to him only a few months earlier and, if anything, it seems to have brought them even closer. Emmet's invited him for even more sleepovers than usual since then, which I think is his way of expressing unqualified support, a move that's impressed me.

'It would be nice to be in a relationship,' I admit, as much to myself as to him. The truth is, all these years,

I genuinely have either been working or bringing him up and haven't had much time to date, although it's not as if there aren't plenty of parents in the class WhatsApp group who would have taken Emmet any time I asked. And a few single mums who've seemed open to the idea of going for drinks. 'I just . . .' I don't know how to finish this sentence. 'Maybe one day,' I say finally.

'Well, don't leave it too late,' he replies, and I'm about to laugh but I can see from the expression on his face that he genuinely means it.

'You don't want me to be alone,' I say quietly.

'I don't want you to be lonely,' he clarifies.

I nod and there's an awkward silence between us.

'I'm sorry about earlier,' he says eventually.

'About what earlier? There's so much to pick from.'

He smiles.

'In the bookshop. Talking about Furia's book like that.'

'Oh. That.'

'It was early. I was tired, hungry and grouchy.'

'It's fine.' I wait a few moments before asking a question that I'm not even sure I want him to answer. 'Have you read it?'

He hesitates for a moment, then shakes his head.

'No.'

'It wouldn't bother me if you had. You like books, and everyone's saying how good it is. You said it had an—'

'Unreliable narrator, I know.'

'That's why I thought you might have. Where did you even pick up such a phrase?'

'In English class. And, you know' – he pauses, takes a sip from his glass – 'in the reviews.'

'You've read the reviews?'

He looks slightly embarrassed. 'A few of them.'

'OK.'

I don't quite know how to feel about this. Was he hoping they'd be negative or positive?

'Have *you* read it?' he asks me, and I give him a look that says, *what do you think?*

It occurs to me that, since he's asking such intimate questions of me, perhaps this is a good opportunity to turn the conversation back on him.

'So, speaking of girlfriends,' I begin, saying each word slowly so as not to frighten him away. 'Is there anyone that you like?'

He opens his eyes wide and looks as if he'd be perfectly happy for the cabin door to burst open right now and suck us both out into the night sky.

'I'm not having this conversation,' he says.

'So, you can ask me about my love life, but I can't ask about yours?'

'Correct,' he says. 'Got it in one.'

'OK, but, joking aside, if there is someone, at school or down the beach or wherever, someone you like, you could talk to me about her.' I sense an opportunity to tease him as he teased me. 'Or about him.'

'You think you're so funny,' he says, rolling his eyes, but he can't help himself, he smiles.

'I do,' I admit.

But while we're on the subject, why do you have semi-naked pictures of yourself on your phone? Who asked for them? Who did you send them to? We've finished our drinks and Noémie asks if we'd like another round. It's completely irresponsible of me, of course, but I see a hopeful look on my son's face, so I nod and say yes. Maybe I'm getting him liquored up so that he might open up to me even more. It's reckless, I suppose, but God knows there are worse things an adult can do to a boy his age. The stewardess gives me a look that says, *I know I've been complicit in this, because the boy charmed me when he told me about your birthday, but this is his last one.*

'What will you do when I'm gone?' he asks when she returns behind the bar.

'Gone?'

'Like, in a few years' time, when I'm out of the house.'

'Why, where are you going?'

'Uni,' he says with a shrug. 'I suppose.'

'Oh right. Then.'

'What will you do?'

I've never given much thought to the fact that it won't be long before I'm back where I started, before I even met Rebecca. It's narcissistic, but the thought flashes through my head that I'm a good man, with a good career. I've kept my body in decent shape, and I'm reasonably attractive. Some might say that I'm a catch. So why the fuck *don't* I have someone, other than my son, to go home to? Why is it that I haven't had sex in so long? Why have I never been to bed with anyone other than my rapist and my ex-wife?

'Dad,' he says, and when I look up, he's staring at me with a concerned expression on his face. 'Dad, what's wrong?'

I shake my head, confused by the question.

'What?' I ask him. 'What do you mean?'

'Dad, you're crying.'

6

Although Rebecca and I were both keen to keep our wedding ceremony small, particularly as I didn't have any family of my own, it surprised me how reluctant she was to extend an invitation to her mother. Some years earlier, Vanessa had spent a year on a small island off the west coast of Ireland and, after returning to the mainland, had quickly emigrated to Boston, where she found work in a library. In time, this led to a position with an independent publishing house. Eighteen months later, she married the director of that company. Rebecca chose not to attend their service, feigning illness, but Vanessa, by contrast, decided to come to ours, flying to England with her new husband in tow and inviting us to dinner in their hotel.

I liked my future mother-in-law immediately. She had a quiet dignity to her, an engaging blend of confidence, vulnerability and mettle. Her short dark hair was peppered with unapologetic grey and, although she was dressed smartly, I guessed she was the sort of woman who cared about her appearance up to a point, but wasn't going to waste too much time worrying about it.

Her and Rebecca's reunion proved predictably uncomfortable, Vanessa reaching in for a hug that was awkwardly received. Introductions followed between stepdaughter and stepfather, a burly American named Ron who came across as a gentle, thoughtful man, and who made an immediate effort with us both. Despite her misgivings and stated intention to remain stand-offish, I could tell that Rebecca grudgingly recognized his sincerity. As a couple, Vanessa and Ron seemed happy, touching each other's arms from time to time and laughing at each other's jokes. Despite being an entire generation older than me, I felt envious of their easy companionship.

It could scarcely have been a more inappropriate thing for me to consider, but I guessed they had a far healthier sex life than Rebecca and I did.

'Are you a reading man, Aaron?' Ron asked me over dinner, and I confessed that I wasn't particularly, that my student years had left me with very little time for anything other than professional textbooks. He asked the same question of Rebecca, who usually had a novel on the go, before producing a small tote bag from beneath the table containing copies of some of the new books he was publishing that season. Years later, I found this same collection on a shelf in our living room and discovered an anthology containing a story by Furia Flyte. When I flicked through it, I discovered notes written in the margins in Rebecca's hand. If she had known at the time of reading the role the author would play in the end of our marriage, I wonder how different those notes might have been.

'I still find it astonishing that you're training to become a pilot,' Vanessa remarked over the main course, and Rebecca, on high alert for anything that might be considered a slight – possibly even hoping for one – bristled.

'Why?' she asked. 'What did you think I should become?'

'It's not that I *thought* you should become anything. It's just that it's an unusual job for a woman, that's all. Historically speaking. When I was a girl, it would have been unthinkable.'

'There was a female pilot on the plane coming over to the UK,' remarked Ron.

'True,' she said, leaning forward and lowering her voice. 'And, of course, the moment she made the announcement – you know the one at the start when the pilot welcomes the passengers and says their name is so and so and the flight time will be however long it will be – there was a groan from some of the men in our cabin. One even said aloud, *I hope you can all swim because we'll be landing in the middle of the Atlantic Ocean*, which he obviously thought was hilarious.'

'She turned around to him,' said Ron, nodding towards his wife proudly.

'I did,' she admitted.

'She told him off.'

'I did!'

'She said, *what's the matter with you? It's not as if she'd be given control of the cockpit if she didn't know the clutch from the brake. Show some respect!*'

'There's no clutch on a plane,' said Rebecca.

'Well, obviously I know nothing about that sort of

thing. But I thought, for heaven's sake, it's the twenty-first century! Do we still have to deal with men who hold such outdated ideas?'

'Personally speaking,' said Ron, 'if I'd had a daughter, it would have knocked my socks off to see her go into a traditionally male industry and show them who was boss.'

'The industry itself isn't traditionally male,' replied Rebecca. 'It's just that over the years the women who've worked within it have mostly been reduced to serving food and drinks.'

'Would you have liked children?' I asked him, and he nodded enthusiastically.

'Oh yes. Very much. I just didn't meet the right woman when I was the right age, that's all. I had my share of relationships, of course, some good, some not so good, but things never seemed to work out for me on that front. Until Vanessa came along, that is.'

He reached across and took her hand, squeezing it gently.

'And by then, we were too old to go down that road.'

'Ron has quite a tight-knit group of nephews and nieces,' said Vanessa. 'They came to the wedding,' she added pointedly. 'They've been very welcoming towards me.'

Rebecca remained silent, forking a carrot and chewing on it meditatively.

'I put all my paternal longings into those kids,' said Ron, and I could see his eyes light up as he described them, two boys and three girls, the lives they were living, the boyfriends and girlfriends they had, the ambitions still before them. One was working in his publishing house and he hoped that she might take it over one day. 'So I've no regrets. I think life works out the way it's supposed to.' He turned to Rebecca now. 'The truth is, I thought I was going to be a confirmed old bachelor for the rest of my days, and I'd made my peace with that, but then I met your mother. I thought I was happy until then. Turned out, I didn't know what happiness really was.'

He looked at Vanessa when he said this, and when she placed a palm gently against his cheek, I felt a strange joy for them. Their affection was so natural and blissful.

Later, they asked where we were hoping to go on our honeymoon and I told them we'd planned four nights in Florence, then three nights in Venice, and Vanessa immediately suggested that we should come to Boston instead.

'The fall is particularly beautiful there,' she added. 'It would be a great time to visit.'

'The fall?' asked Rebecca, in as sarcastic a tone as she could muster. 'You mean the autumn, right?'

'Sorry,' she said, laughing a little. 'I've turned into such a native. I say things like *sidewalk* and *elevator* these days.'

'And *dude*,' added Ron, and Vanessa turned to him in outrage, denying that she'd ever called anyone *dude* in her entire life, but then he made a reference to a young writer whose publicity campaign she'd been working on, and she admitted that yes, she might have called him *dude* once, but she'd had one too many Cosmopolitans at the time so it shouldn't be held against her.

'He won a Pulitzer, you know,' added Ron.

'Who did?' asked Rebecca.

'The writer,' he told us. 'In no small part because of

your mother's hard work. You should be very proud of her. She's a smart cookie.'

Vanessa remained silent throughout this commendation, taking a sip from her glass of wine, her cheeks flushing a little. I could tell that she was pleased by the compliment, and proud that it was clearly deserved.

'It's like you're a different human being entirely,' said Rebecca, and it was difficult to tell from her tone whether she meant this in a positive or negative way.

'How do you mean?'

'It's hard to say,' she replied, shaking her head. 'It's like you're not Vanessa Carvin any more. Not the one I grew up with, anyway. You look like her, for the most part. And you talk like her. But you're different.'

'Well, many years have passed, so naturally I've changed. It happens.'

'You're not even Willow Hale.'

I turned to look at Rebecca, uncertain what she meant by this, and Vanessa exhaled a small, sad sigh.

'I'm surprised you even remember that name,' she said.

'Who's Willow Hale?' I asked.

'Willow Hale was the name my mother assumed when she ran away and left me.'

'I didn't run away and leave you, Rebecca,' replied Vanessa in a measured tone. 'If anything, I ran away and left *me*. And I messaged you constantly. I woke up every morning wondering whether your picture would still be on my contacts list or not. If her picture was there, Aaron,' she said, turning to me, 'it meant that she was open to me messaging her. If it was gone, then she'd blocked me. It was very random from one day to the next. Honestly, there were times I didn't even want to look because of how hurtful it could be.'

I turned to look at Rebecca, but she didn't meet my eyes. She'd told me about the island, and why her mother had gone there, but not about her pseudonym or their lack of interaction during that period.

'I came to visit,' she said.

'You did,' agreed Vanessa. 'For a night.'

'What was it like?' I asked. 'The island, I mean.'

Vanessa breathed in deeply and I could tell that she was searching for the right way to describe it.

'Life-changing,' she said eventually. 'Peaceful. Full of strange, wonderful, difficult people. I'm not sure that I'd be sitting here today if I hadn't gone there.'

Our small group fell silent then and finally, to break the tension, Ron asked about my plans for the future. I told him that I hoped to work with children who'd suffered some form of trauma in their lives.

'And you'll stay here?' he asked.

'We haven't made a decision about that yet.'

'It's an expensive city, from what I'm told. Especially if you plan on having children.'

'We don't,' said Rebecca decisively, which was news to me, and I realized that we'd never discussed the topic of becoming parents. I suppose I'd always taken it for granted that this would happen in time. I turned to look at her, trying to keep the surprise off my face, and she deliberately stared into the bowl of her wine glass, swilling the contents just enough that they touched the peak of the rim without spilling over.

'I couldn't bring a child into this world,' she continued. 'I just couldn't. I think about what your first husband did' – Rebecca never referred to Brendan as her father, just as her mother's first husband – 'and I think about what happened to Aaron when he was a boy—'

'What happened to you when you were a boy?' asked Vanessa, looking at me.

'And I simply refuse to bring another human into such a world. If he or she could just be born as an adult, then that would be fine. But they have to go through childhood first, don't they? And one way or another, someone will fuck them up. Or just fuck them.'

Vanessa muttered something under her breath and looked away, her jaw tightening. I sensed there were emotions that she wanted to express but that she was uncertain how they might be received. Ron took a sip from his beer while I stared down at my meal. Eventually, Vanessa repeated her question and, in as brief a way as possible, keeping my language plain so as not to turn the evening any darker than it had already become, I explained what had taken place in my life when I was fourteen.

I know he meant well.

I know he was only trying to lighten the mood.

I know he simply didn't understand the experience I had gone through, but that was when Ron said:

'Jesus. When I was that age, I would have given my left arm to be seduced by an older woman.'

The moment the words were out of his mouth, I think even he knew that he'd said the wrong thing. Vanessa froze, as did Rebecca. He closed his eyes, and they remained that way for about ten seconds while everyone at the table remained silent. 'I'm so sorry,' he said at last. 'That was such a dumb thing to say. Obviously, I have no understanding of what you went through or the effect it had on you.'

'He didn't say he was *seduced* by an older woman,' said Rebecca, her voice rising now, her tone enraged. I noticed a couple at a nearby table turning to look in our direction. 'He said he was *raped* by one. There's a big fucking difference, *Ron*.'

'I'm very sorry,' he repeated, reaching his enormous hand across the table and placing it atop mine, an intimate gesture that I found strangely comforting. 'I'm a big stupid American who speaks before he thinks.'

'It's fine,' I told him, because I knew that his apology was sincere. I'd heard men say things like this before. The same men who would insist that if a thirty-two-year-old man even glanced in a lascivious way towards their fourteen-year-old daughter, they would gladly serve a life sentence for their murder.

Vanessa took her husband's left hand, leaving three of us physically connected. Only Rebecca held herself apart.

'I'm sorry, sweetheart,' Ron whispered to his wife, and she gave him a quick kiss as he looked around the table, his brow furrowed. 'I know what Vanessa suffered. And, of course, I know what happened to Emma. So it's not something to make light of. Maybe that's one of the things that brought you two together?'

Oh Ron, I thought. *Stop speaking. Please stop speaking.*

Rebecca put her glass down, firmly, and placed her hand against her forehead, holding it there.

'It's a terrible world we live in,' he continued. 'I had such a happy childhood myself. I hope you've found a way to make peace with what happened to you, Aaron.'

'Well, I try not to allow it to affect my life any deeper than it already has,' I replied quietly.

'That seems very sensible,' said Vanessa. 'If you don't mind me asking, what happened to the woman? Did you report her?'

'Only a couple of years ago. By which time, she'd done a lot of damage to other boys. I should have done it earlier.'

'You can't blame yourself for that.'

'I know, but I regret my delay.'

'And was she punished?'

'Yes. Arrested, charged, tried and incarcerated. She admitted to it all. And worse.'

'What could be worse?'

'Suffice to say she won't be setting foot outside prison again in her lifetime.'

'Well, that's something.'

'Please don't ever mention my sister's name again,' said Rebecca quietly, looking down at the table. Her tone made it clear that she'd spent the last couple of minutes seething over Ron's remarks.

'Rebecca,' said Vanessa.

'I mean it. You didn't know her. You never met her. So please don't speak about her as if you have any under-standing of who she was or what we lost.'

I turned to her, pleading with my eyes for her to stop, but her attention was focused solely on him.

'I won't,' he replied, his tone entirely sincere. 'And I apologize for doing so. I didn't realize it would upset you this much, but I do now and will keep it in mind in the future.'

I could feel the tension in her simmering away, long-ing to boil over. Her fury that he was being so reasonable and refusing to participate in an argument. She wanted to tear into him, this substitute father, someone who might soak up the rage she felt towards her real one, but he simply wasn't giving her the opportunity.

'Perhaps Aaron and I should go for a drink in the bar,' he suggested finally, looking down at our plates, which were empty now. 'You two ladies haven't seen each other in so long. You could probably do with a little time to catch up without us boys getting in the way.'

I felt a sense of relief when Vanessa nodded.

It was more than an hour later before she rejoined us, telling me that Rebecca was waiting for me in the lobby.

'She's not coming in to say goodbye?' I asked, and she shook her head.

'No, she just wants to go home.'

I said my goodbyes to both and made my way towards the door. Before I could leave, however, Vanessa caught up with me.

'Aaron,' she said, standing close to me, 'I want you to

know that I love my daughter very much. I would lay down my life for her if I had to. And obviously I've only just met you for the first time tonight, but from what I've observed, you seem like a kind, thoughtful young man. She's lucky to have you. But, out of consideration to you, can I offer you one piece of advice?'

'Of course,' I said.

She took both my hands in hers, clutching them tightly, and looked me directly in my eyes.

'Don't marry her,' she said. 'You're a fool if you do.'

7

WE BOTH SLEEP THROUGH the last few hours of the Dubai flight and emerge, slightly groggy, into the airport, where we shuffle towards our next gate for the short layover. Slumped in our seats, I'm scrolling through my phone, while Emmet is staring into the distance, lost in thought. His hair is a mess and he's compulsively running his fingers through it, giving off a definite air of anxiety.

Without a word, he wanders off to the bathroom, leaving his bag and phone on the seat next to me, and, a minute or so later, when it buzzes, I glance towards it, where a message from Damian has popped up. *U made ur mind up yet?* it says, and I frown but don't touch it. If I did, Emmet would surely reappear just as I'm looking at it. Still, I can't help but wonder what he's referring to. It doesn't take long for me to find out, however, for when my son returns, he has a rather determined expression on his face. He sits down, looks at the phone for a moment, reads the message, taps a quick reply, then puts it in his pocket before clearing his throat. When he speaks, his tone suggests that he's been thinking about what he's about to say for some time and is fully prepared for an argument.

'Dad,' he says.

'What's up?'

'There's something I need to tell you.'

'OK.'

'Only you can't be angry with me.'

Perhaps he wants to talk about the pictures on his phone. It's not the ideal time to discuss them, but it would certainly be a lot easier if he brought the topic up rather than me having to introduce it. I've spent more than a year counselling a boy only slightly older than him who gave in to a sextortion scam on Snapchat, clearing almost three thousand dollars from his parents' bank account before they discovered what was going on and reported the incident to the police. Although, thankfully, the pictures and videos he sent to his blackmailer never made it into the public domain or to his list of contacts, as had been threatened, he remains utterly traumatized by the incident, which went on for months, and a chill spreads through me as I wonder whether Emmet has found himself in a similar situation.

'Go on,' I say.

'No, you have to promise.'

'Just tell me.'

He takes a deep breath, then exhales slowly.

'I'm not getting on this plane.'

Of everything I might have anticipated, this never occurred to me. But at least it's not as bad as what it might have been.

'I'm sorry?'

'I said I'm not getting on this plane. I'm not going any further. I'm staying here.'

I turn to look at him, to see whether he's serious. If there's one thing I've learned over the years from my patients, it's the importance of remaining calm when someone says something that is clearly designed for a reaction.

'Emmet,' I say, glancing at my watch, 'boarding is due to start in about fifteen minutes, so you don't really have much choice. We've done the long part of the flight already. This is the shorter one. We'll be there before you know it.'

'It's not about the length of the journey,' he tells me. 'I'm just not going, it's as simple as that. You go if you want to. But I'm staying here.'

'What, here in the airport? For the next five nights?'

'You can book me a hotel room,' he says. 'It's Dubai. There's thousands of them.'

'And five nights in one of them would cost more than this entire trip.'

'Oh, please,' he says, rolling his eyes. 'You're loaded.'

'I'm not loaded,' I say. 'But that's hardly the point. I'm not leaving you on your own in a strange city. We agreed to make this trip together, remember, you and me? We have to be there for her.'

'Why?' he asks.

'Why what?'

'Why do we have to be there for her?'

It takes me a moment to come up with what I realize is an unsatisfactory, and possibly dishonest, answer.

'Because if things were the other way around, she'd be there for you.'

'Like she's been in the past, you mean?'

He throws his head far back over the seat, staring up at the ceiling, remaining silent for a moment, as if he can't quite comprehend the duplicity of adults. I know he's telling himself that he'll never be the same when he's older. But he will. We all are.

'You see your mother regularly,' I tell him, and he laughs bitterly.

'I see her once or twice a year at most,' he replies. 'It's not like she goes out of her way to spend time with me.'

'You spend a month with her.'

'Wrong. I come here for a month, but I spend most of it sitting on my own in her apartment, reading books, watching movies, or down in the pool, while she's flying around somewhere. When she does bother to show up, she's either too tired to hang out with me or can't think of anything for us to do. Last time, she came back from Singapore after three days away and seemed to forget that I was even staying there. I literally came out of my bedroom to say hello and she screamed like I was a burglar. I swear, it took her a minute even to recognize me.'

'She was probably jetlagged, that's all.'

'Pilots don't get jetlagged,' he replies with utter certainty, and I have no idea whether this is true or just something he's read online.

'She's your mother,' I say.

'No. She's your ex-wife. There's a difference.'

I can only imagine how deeply it would hurt Rebecca if she heard this remark – it reminds me of how she always referred to Brendan as Vanessa's ex-husband – and there's a part of me that wishes she had. Because as fortunate as I've felt at being my son's primary guardian, it's shocked me how small a part Rebecca has played in his upbringing.

Emmet was only four years old when the whole mess with Furia led to the end of our marriage. When it became clear that the infidelity would prove to be the closing act of our relationship, the plan had been that Rebecca would remain in Sydney and he would divide his time between us. I had grown to love Australia, my practice was there, and I had neither reason nor inclination to return to the northern hemisphere. And for the first twelve months, this arrangement worked reasonably well. But when the airline reorganized its pilot schedule, it made more sense for her to relocate to their hub in Dubai, and I was worried that she'd want to take Emmet with her. He was settled in school, had his circle of close friends, was thriving at Bondi's Nippers Club, and I felt it would be cruel to remove him from that. The pain of the betrayal had left things raw between us, however, and I was uncertain how Rebecca would respond to my suggestion that Emmet remain in my custody full-time, assuming she'd refuse, but to my surprise, she agreed, even expressing a sense of relief that she was free to live her own life. While her selfishness troubled me, I had no intention of challenging her on it. After all, had she insisted on taking him, and had the courts permitted her to do so, I would have had no choice but to follow her. But no, she just left him.

Last year was the first time Emmet asked whether he

could cancel his visit – he was distraught at the idea of being torn away from his beloved beach over Christmas – and I used my dwindling authority to insist that he go, because I wanted him to maintain a relationship with his mother. I'd already anticipated that he would put up more of a fight this coming year, and that, at fifteen, he might even win, but because of the circumstances that have brought us to this airport now, I assume that visit won't be happening anyway.

Ahead, I notice an airline employee preparing the desk and another relocating the stanchions that separate the queues for First, Business and Economy passengers. There's simply no way that I'm leaving him here alone.

'Emmet—' I begin, but he raises a hand and cuts me off.

'I mean it,' he says. 'Honestly, Dad, this isn't a sudden decision. I've been thinking about it ever since we boarded in Sydney.'

'Oh, that long? Wow. A whole thirteen hours.'

'And I don't want to go any further. Look, I know Dubai pretty well and I'm not a little kid any more. All you need to do is book someplace on your phone. You can do it right now; there's free Wi-Fi. It doesn't have to be any place fancy.' He smiles a little, hoping to charm me. 'I mean, not a dive though. A pool would be nice.'

'A pool would be lovely,' I agree. 'As would a penthouse suite, a gym, a sauna, a massage and twenty-four-hour room service. But none of those things are going to happen.'

'Not for you, maybe.'

'Not for you either.'

'I'll be fine,' he says, looking me directly in the eye. 'I'm fourteen.'

'When you say *I'm fourteen*,' I tell him, 'my response is *you're* only *fourteen*. The preposition matters.'

'"Only" isn't a preposition,' he says. 'It's an adverb.'

He's probably right. He's the reader, after all, not me. Around us, I can tell that the other passengers are sensing the impending boarding announcement as they're starting to gather their things, preparing to rush the gate like a pack of feral dogs the moment someone so much as taps the microphone.

'Can I be really honest with you about something?' says Emmet, and I nod.

'Of course.'

'And you'll hear me out?'

'I'll hear you out.'

He takes a deep breath and points towards the gate. 'There is nothing, absolutely nothing, that will make me get on that plane,' he says. 'Nothing you can say, nothing you can do. If you cause a fuss, I'll throw some sort of fit and Security will have us both removed. So it's this simple: you can organize a hotel room for me and go on to Ireland alone, or we can both return to Sydney right now, together. It's your choice. I'm sorry. I had planned on seeing it through. Honestly, I had. And I feel bad about leaving you to do this without me. This isn't something I planned and I'm not trying to let you down. Especially today. On your birthday. If it's still your birthday.' He pauses for a moment and frowns. 'Is it still your birthday?' he asks. 'I mean, with the time difference, is it still today? Or yesterday? Or—'

'Emmet!' I snap. Global time zones are the last thing on my mind right now.

'Sorry. OK. Anyway, my point is I don't see why I should give her this when she's given me nothing.'

'Other than life, you mean.'

He crosses his arms defensively and shakes his head. I've dealt with a lot of children and teenagers throughout my career, and they can be difficult in any one of a thousand ways. Another parent might panic at a declaration like this and, I will admit, I'm starting to grow unnerved as we're under severe time pressure. But I have to remain calm.

'You must want a better relationship with her,' I say.

'I used to. I don't really care any more.'

'Don't say that.'

'Why not?'

'Look, she's a complicated woman. You don't know what she's been through.'

He laughs. 'What?' he asks sarcastically. 'What has she been through? As far as I can see, she's done everything her way, always. Made her own decisions. Let us both down.'

I remain silent. Of course, he knows nothing about the realities of Rebecca's past. We've both kept that from him.

'She doesn't love me, Dad,' he continues, and I can see tears forming in his eyes. 'Not like you love me.'

'She does,' I insist. 'She just doesn't know how to express it, that's all. She's damaged. We're both damaged.'

'You're not.'

'I am, Emmet.'

'How?' he asks, sounding intrigued now, perhaps hearing something in my tone that tells him that he might not know me quite as well as he thinks he does, but I shake my head.

'That's a conversation for another time,' I say. 'Right now, we have bigger things to worry about. We have to go. We *have* to.'

'Why?'

'Because – Jesus! – I loved her once, Emmet, that's why. Very much. Very deeply. We got married. We planned a life together. And we created you.'

'So you go, then. You be there for her if it's so important to you.'

'Not without you. No. I know you're angry with her but—'

'I have no feelings about her one way or the other,' he says, the crack in his voice showing that he's almost overwhelmed by the complexity of his emotions and his inability to negotiate them. The jetlag is probably only adding to his stress.

'And you have every reason to feel that way,' I continue calmly. 'But trust me, now is not the time to act upon those feelings. This is a moment in life when your mother needs you. She needs both of us, whether she realizes it or not. And she will be glad that we're there.'

He stares at me. I sense a chink in his armour. I've found myself in moments like this before, in professional settings, and know that I just need to prise it open. Very carefully.

'The loss of a parent can cause people to think differently about their lives,' I tell him. 'I've seen it many times in my work.'

'You work with children.'

'And sometimes children lose their parents. Jacob lost Jackie, remember?'

He looks away and swallows, considering this. Jacob is one of his closest friends, part of the gang he hangs around with at the beach, a boy who's spent countless nights sleeping in the top bunk in Emmet's bedroom since they were kids. His mother passed away from cancer just over a year ago and Jacob has handled his grief admirably.

'I remember,' he says.

'And you were there for him. You and Damian. And Shane and Maxie. I've watched you all. I've seen how much you've helped him.'

'Cos he's our friend.'

'And Rebecca's your mum. She'll be thinking about you now, I know she will.'

He turns to look at me. He wants reassurance.

'How do you know that?' he asks.

'Because I understand people. I'm trained to understand them. It's the one thing I know I can do well.'

What feels like an endless silence lingers between us and, when he speaks again, his determination seems to have diminished a little.

'If she'd wanted us to come,' he says, 'wouldn't she have said so?'

'That's not her way. You don't know her like I do.'

'Of course I don't,' he says, bursting into a bitter laugh. 'I barely know her at all. That's the problem.'

'And this is an opportunity to start rectifying that.'

'That's on her, not me.'

'You're right. You are absolutely right. And one day, I have no doubt that you and she will sit down and discuss your relationship. When that day comes, you'll be able to tell her that you flew halfway across the world at this crucial moment because you wanted to support her. I'm not trying to pit you against each other, you know I've never done that, but trust me, that is a card you'll be able to pull out of your deck when the moment arrives.'

'I shouldn't need a fucking card,' he whispers, wiping tears away now. He's an emotional boy, he always has been, but he hasn't cried in front of me in a long time. When something upsets him, he tends to take to his room.

'No, you shouldn't,' I agree, knowing that I can't put an arm around him, even though I want to. To pull him close would be to push him away. 'But you have one.'

'She didn't even speak to me on the phone,' he says, his tone softening.

'Perhaps she was worried that you'd say no to coming.'

'I would have said yes.'

'And you *did* say yes. You said yes when I told you what had happened. When I suggested we go over. You said yes then.'

'Only because I knew you wouldn't have let me stay home alone. Even though I'm fourteen.'

'*Only* fourteen,' I repeat. 'The preposition—'

'Adverb!'

'Jesus, fine! The adverb! The point is, you *did* agree, Emmet. You agreed instantly. You want to go; I know you do. Even if you're nervous about what awaits us at the other end. You want to be there for her.'

The announcement comes. First-class passengers can board now. We still have a few minutes until Business is called.

'No,' he says, looking down at the floor.

In front of us, I notice another family, a husband, wife and a boy about my son's age, stand up and gather their hand luggage. They look so full of energy and excitement that I assume they're travelling directly from Dubai and haven't endured a thirteen-hour flight already. As they leave their seats, the mother throws an arm around her son's shoulder, kisses him on the cheek, and they walk on together in perfect contentment. The boy turns to her to say something, and she bursts out laughing. I see Emmet watching them too and he looks desolate.

Once again, he points at the gate.

'I'm sorry, Dad,' he says, shaking his head. 'I really am. I promise, I'm not doing this to hurt you. Or to hurt her. But there is absolutely no way that I'm getting on that plane to Dublin. None. You either book me a hotel here, a flight home, or I just sleep in this airport for the next five nights. It's up to you.'

8

WE HAD ONLY BEEN back in England from our honeymoon a few months when we received an unexpected visitor. I was reading through some case notes at home when the doorbell rang and I opened it to find a man standing outside, in his early seventies I judged, with a slim build and a few scraps of grey hair dragged mercilessly across his crown.

'You must be Aaron,' he said, and I was a little taken aback that a stranger should know my name.

'I am,' I said.

He extended a hand. 'We haven't met,' he said. 'I'm Daniel. I work with your wife at the airline. Nothing as exciting as what she does, I'm afraid. You wouldn't be safe with me in the cockpit! No, I'm in Human Resources. I'm sorry to drop by unannounced, but there were a few documents that I needed her to sign and I'm away on holiday for the next two weeks and, since your house was on my way home, I—'

'Oh right, of course,' I said, standing back and ushering him inside. 'Sorry, please come in. She's just taking a bath though, so it might be a few minutes.'

'No problem. I'm happy to wait if you're happy to have me.'

We made our way into the living room and I tried not to notice how carefully he studied everything in the room – the books on the shelves, the paintings on the wall, the magazines on the coffee table – as if he was considering renting a room from us.

'Very nice,' he said quietly, more to himself than me. 'Very nice indeed.'

'Can I make you a cup of tea?' I asked.

'You could, yes, but would it be very rude if I asked for something a little stronger? Only it's fierce cold out there tonight and I'm not as young as I used to be.'

'I might have a beer in the fridge,' I said.

'Maybe a whiskey?'

It seemed like a slightly forward request from a guest, but I offered to look, walking into the kitchen, where, hidden away at the back of a cupboard, I found an unopened bottle of Bushmills.

'Water? Ice?' I asked, standing in the doorway and displaying it to him.

'We won't disgrace it with dilution,' he said, and I poured him a glass, neat, bringing it back with me and leaving the bottle on the table between us. The scent of it, one I rarely experienced, brought me back to my childhood, to my own father, who had always enjoyed a glass of Glenfiddich on Friday nights when I was a child. It was a comforting memory.

'You won't join me?' he asked, and I shook my head.

'Better not,' I said. 'Work in the morning.'

'Did no one ever tell you that it's the height of bad manners to leave a man drinking alone in your home?'

His tone was just on the polite side of confrontational, and he wore such a disturbing smile that I was left feeling rather unsettled. He continued to stare without so much as raising his glass to his lips so, when I realized that he actually meant it, I returned to the kitchen and took a bottle of Heineken from the fridge.

'That's much better,' he said when I returned. 'I can enjoy my drink now. You have a lovely home,' he added, looking around.

'Thank you,' I said. 'We're only renting, of course, but in time—'

'Wasted money.'

'I'm sorry?'

'I said, wasted money. Filling a landlord's pockets when you could be paying your own mortgage.'

I looked at him, uncertain how to respond to this.

'When I was a young man,' he continued, 'when I married, there was no such thing as renting. I went from my parents' house to my marital home. I never gave a penny to anyone else, other than the banks, who fleeced me, of course, because that's the nature of the beast, but I paid it all off before I turned fifty and then what was mine was mine. Or at least I thought it was.'

I was glad of the Heineken now and took a long swig from it, feeling a slight sense of relief that there were a few more in the door of the fridge if I needed them.

'You're a doctor,' he asked after a moment. 'Did I hear that about you?'

'I am, yes.'

'What kind of a doctor, if you don't mind me asking?'

'Psychology. Child psychology, to be precise.'

'Child psychology,' he said, musing on this. 'Freud,' he added, apropos of nothing.

'Well, Freud was a psychoanalyst,' I replied. 'I'm more of a—'

'Obsessed with sex, wasn't he? Freud, I mean.'

I shrugged.

'I think that's rather a clichéd notion of his philosophies, to be honest.'

'Thought everyone wanted to murder their father and sleep with their mother. Like that lad over beyond in Denmark.'

I stared at him, uncertain to whom he was referring. Was there some appalling psychopath emerging from Copenhagen that I'd missed out on?

'Hamlet,' he said, leaning forward and enunciating the word carefully, as if he was on the stage of the Globe itself.

'Oh right,' I replied. 'Of course. Yes.'

'Can I ask you a personal question? Is there good money in psychology? Or child psychology?'

I didn't quite know how to answer such a peculiar question.

'Relative to what?' I asked.

'Oh, I don't know,' he replied. 'Relative to being a GP, for example.'

'Well, it's not really about the pay scales,' I told him. 'We all know the NHS runs on too little as it is.

Everyone says how much they love it, but no one wants to pay for it.'

'Would you not think of going private, no?' he asked, and I realized now that he was Irish, although his accent was not particularly strong. 'Would there not be more money in that?'

'No, I don't approve of private healthcare.'

'Do you not?' he said, raising an eyebrow. 'May I ask why?'

'Because I don't believe that patient care should depend on a person's wealth. Especially when it comes to the well-being of children. Every person has the right to the same level of support, regardless of their circumstances.'

'You don't think that if a man, for example, has worked hard all his life and earned a good living that he should be entitled to spend his money any way he wants?'

'Sure,' I replied. 'And if he wants to spend it on luxury hotels, first-class flights, fancy cars or a season ticket to his favourite football club, then I say good luck to him. But should he be allowed to jump the queue for medical attention? I think that's a bit more complicated. Morally speaking, I mean.'

'That sounds like socialism to me,' he replied, frowning. 'Which, in my experience, is a luxury only those with a few quid in the bank can afford. But then, perhaps you're one of those very people.'

'I think, perhaps, you overestimate our financial situation,' I said, trying to sound light-hearted, and he glanced around again, a raised eyebrow suggesting that

JOHN BOYNE

he wasn't sure he was. Our home might have been rented, but it was in a good part of North London, after all, and was expensively furnished. My parents had owned their house and been scrupulous savers, and so, when they died, I inherited more than enough to get a good start in life. The only reason we were still renting was because we hadn't yet decided whether we wanted to remain in London or move abroad.

'In a perfect world,' said Daniel, 'you must wish you were unemployed.'

I sat back, baffled by why he would say such a thing.

'Because,' he continued, sensing my confusion, 'if no one had any need of you, then all the little children would be happy. There'd be no one looking for the help of a child psychologist.'

I thought about it. It was, to be fair, a reasonable point, one I'd never considered before.

'You don't have children yourself, do you, Aaron?' he asked, and I shook my head. 'When you do, you might have a different attitude about private healthcare. Should one of those children fall ill, God forbid, you would want them to receive treatment as soon as possible. Even if it meant that some poor unfortunate child who'd been ahead of you in the queue got left behind. It's human nature. We look after our own first.'

I could have protested but suspected he was probably right. I wasn't naïve enough to think that principles had a peculiar habit of disappearing when confronted by brutal reality.

'By what you say, I assume you're a father,' I said,

hoping to lighten the mood. He finished his whiskey and held his glass out to me with a smile. I took this as his signal that he wanted another, so lifted the bottle and duly refilled it.

'I am,' he said, his voice quieter now, more reflective. 'I was blessed with two but, sadly, we lost one.'

'I'm sorry to hear that.'

'There is nothing more unnatural in this world,' he said, looking directly at me and pointing a finger in the air, '*nothing* more unnatural than for a parent to lose a child. No man or woman should ever have to experience that level of grief.'

'No,' I agreed, glancing towards the closed door that led to a corridor which, in turn, divided our bedroom and spare room on one side from the bathroom on the other. I hoped to hear the water rushing from the bath, knowing the sound would bring Rebecca to us within a few minutes.

'And are your parents still alive, Aaron?' he called after me when I went back to the kitchen to retrieve a second beer for myself.

'No,' I replied, when I returned.

'They must have died young.'

'My father suffered a heart attack in his forties. My mother developed cancer a few years later and, unfortunately, it was late stage by the time it was diagnosed.'

'Siblings?'

I shook my head.

'So you're all alone in the world.'

'No,' I said. 'I have Rebecca.'

'Of course, of course,' he replied, nodding his head.

'But you have no one of your own to fall back on.'

'Again, Rebecca.'

'No one of your own blood, I mean.'

I sighed. He seemed determined to have his way on this. 'I suppose not,' I said.

'The little boy that Santa Claus forgot.'

I frowned. I had never thought of myself in quite those terms before.

'It's a good thing you met Rebecca so,' he said. 'She's a wonderful young woman.'

'She is,' I agreed.

'Can I ask you a personal question?'

This was the second time he had asked this, and I felt we'd already gone well past polite small talk but nodded cautiously.

'If you had to describe your late parents in a single word, what word would that be?'

I thought about this for a little before answering.

'Successful,' I said eventually.

'Now that's a very strange reply,' he said. 'Successful in what way? In their work?'

'In a sense. You said that the worst thing that can happen to any man or woman is to lose a child, and I don't disagree with you on that. But, by the same token, the best thing that any man or woman can do in life is to be a good parent. To give their children a happy child-hood. And my parents did that. They were kind people. They loved me, they took care of me. Always made me feel worthwhile.' Perhaps the beer was getting to me because I added: 'There was a time, in my teens, when I struggled with life. During those years, I wasn't always as kind to them as I might have been. But they never pushed me away. They were always in my corner, even when I gave them cause to run far from it. So the reason I say "successful" is because they took on the most important role in the world and did a great job at it.'

He nodded his head. 'Now that's a lovely thing to say,' he told me. 'And if they're listening from up there in heaven, then I imagine they'll have a smile on their faces hearing such generous words. I only hope my daughter, my surviving daughter that is, will be able to say the same thing about me some day. And that, in time, when you're a parent yourself, you'll follow their example.'

'I hope so,' I said. Since our night out with Vanessa and Ron around the time of our wedding, Rebecca and I had never discussed her comments regarding not wanting to bring a child into the world. We should have, of course, but I hoped that it had simply been a throwaway remark, one designed to hurt her mother. I still assumed that one day we would have kids of our own. Although, of course, to have a child would require actually having sex.

'Still, at least you're married,' continued Daniel, betraying a little more of his accent now. 'Which is the right way to be. All these girls today having babies with no sign of a ring on their fingers. There's a cheapness to them, don't you think? A lack of self-respect.'

'I don't think people care about those sorts of things any more,' I said.

'That's because the young behave like animals,' he replied, leaning forward, his face darkening. 'And we allow it. God created marriage for a reason.'

'God didn't create marriage,' I told him. 'Man did.'

He waved this away dismissively.

'A child should have a father and a mother,' he insisted. 'And that father and mother should be joined in the sacrament of marriage, a sacrament, I might add, that no court order can dissolve, even if the world thinks otherwise. Don't you agree with me, Aaron?'

'No,' I said firmly. 'If a child has two parents who love each other and remain together, then that's obviously a good thing, but whether they're married or not seems neither here nor there. And a parent can bring up a child alone and do a great job. Ultimately, it's about love.'

'My wife and I waited,' he told me, tapping a finger against his nose, as if I was to keep this piece of intelligence to myself. He poured himself another healthy shot of the whiskey and held it to the light, looking at it admiringly. 'Or rather, I waited. She had a history, I'm sorry to say. One that I was willing to overlook, which is as much to my shame as it is to hers. When I met her, she'd already been with other men. Only a few, she told me, but who's to say? Women lie. You know that as well as I do. It's in their nature. They are inherently deceitful. Especially when they're trying to trap a man, and she trapped me well and good, so she did. Oh, for a stupid woman, she was very clever when it came to snaring her catch. It took a long time for us to conceive a child, and it wasn't for want of trying, oh no. Let me assure you,

Aaron, that relations between us in those early years were as regular as they were convivial, but month after month we were left disappointed. Let's go to a doctor, she said, and I did as I was told because is there anything that a man wants more than a quiet life? So we went to the doctor, a lady doctor, mind you, and didn't she – the lady doctor, I mean, not my wife – didn't she suggest that it might be my fault that we were having no success. If I wasn't a man who'd been brought up to respect the fairer sex, I'd have given her a good slap for her troubles, and there wouldn't have been a jury in the land that—'

He broke off for a moment when he said this and took a long breath, closing his eyes. I allowed the silence to linger, not wishing to say anything.

'Anyway, rest assured, I never laid a hand on her. And, as it turned out, it wasn't my fault at all. There was nothing wrong with me. Or her, in fact. It was just God's way of making us wait so that we would love our children even more when they finally arrived. And He knows that we treated those girls like they were princesses of the royal blood. There was never, let me tell you, two little girls who were loved more.'

He took a longer swig from the whiskey now, and I could tell that he was growing drunk. Somewhere at the back of my mind, an idea started to suggest itself to me, but, like a ship lost at sea on a dark night, it was still partly hidden by fog.

'When you do have children, Aaron,' he said, 'may the good Lord see fit to bless you with sons. What is it that fella in *The Godfather* says, when he visits the Don at the wedding? The lad who ends up sleeping with the fishes. *May your first child be a masculine child!* Good strong boys who can look up to you and take after you. I loved my girls, I did, but a house full of women with their potions and their notions, their concoctions and their gossiping, and their bras and their panties hanging out on the washing line every afternoon, it can be too much for a man. A taunt. Something to get him all riled up. No, a man needs sons, that's the truth of it. And a man like me, in my position, with all I had to give, should have had sons. Sons would have stood up for me in my hour of need and not abandoned me like the women in my life did. That woman I called a wife and those girls I called daughters and who made up the most despicable lies about me. Have you ever had someone make up a despicable lie about you, Aaron? Have you ever had to endure a calumny that blackens your name and your reputation for ever? There is nothing worse, let me tell you. When someone says that you've done a thing that you would never in a million years do, not unless you were invited to anyway, and the world hears about it and it turns on you and it says abominable things, well, it's like no other form of torture. You won't have had that happen to you, of course not, you're just a young man yet, but in time you might, so if you become a father, and I hope you do, then please God, may your first child be a—'

I sprang to my feet, upsetting the table, and he reared back, looking at me in surprise.

'Get out,' I said, a feeling of nausea overwhelming me as I finally realized who my visitor was and that he had no more connection to Rebecca's airline than I did. To my right, I heard the bathroom door open, then the bedroom door, and knew that Rebecca would be with us shortly.

'But why should I leave?' the man asked, holding his hands out to me like a supplicant. 'A man has a right to see his daughter.'

'You lost all your rights after what you did.'

'Eleven years rotting away in Midlands Prison with nothing to do but stare at the four walls all day and try to get from breakfast to dinner without having the head beaten off me by murderers and rapists and drug dealers because they needed someone to look down on, and who else only Muggins here, Muggins who was stitched up by his whore of a wife and his slut of a daughter, who he'd given everything to, who he'd worked every day of his life for, and who abandoned him when he needed them the most. Don't you think after something like that happens that a man has a right to look that bitch in the eye and ask, why did you do that, darling girl, why did you do that to me? Don't you know that everything I ever did was for you and your sister, that I loved you both, that I would have laid down my life for—'

The door opened and Rebecca stepped into the living room in oversized pyjamas, running a towel through her wet hair.

'Are you hungry?' she asked. 'I feel like some Thai food if you—'

She paused, obviously surprised to find someone else in the room with me, probably embarrassed that he would discover her in her nightwear, and I could tell that it took a few moments for her brain to catch up with her eyes and recognize who had invaded her place of safety under false pretences.

Her scream was a sound that haunts me still.

9

WHETHER IT WAS MY argument about Jacob's late mother, my suggestion that he would one day be able to express to Rebecca how he'd been present when she most needed him, my refusal to book him a five-night stay in a Dubai hotel, or the exasperated tone of an unimpressed airline representative telling us that the doors would be closed in the next sixty seconds with or without us, Emmet finally agrees to board the plane. Throwing his hands in the air, he offers a series of furious expletives and storms ahead of me, taking his seat without another word.

This time, we're on opposite sides of the cabin so don't have to interact during the flight, which is probably for the best. Once we're in the air, I stand up to look across and see that he's immersed in another film, a blanket pulled over his body so only his eyes and the top of his head are visible. With the exception of a couple of trips to the bathroom, when we pass by without even acknowledging each other's existence, neither of us leaves our seats until we land in Ireland just over seven hours later.

It's early afternoon when we arrive at our hotel in the

centre of Dublin. As we've been travelling for twenty-four hours, I've reserved a room here for the night, so we can rest before undertaking the final leg of our journey. When we step inside, Emmet stares at the two single beds with a frown before turning and asking for his key.

'Here,' I say, handing him one of the cards the receptionist gave me when we checked in.

'What's my room number?'

'I'm sorry?'

'My room number. Or is this one mine?'

It takes me a moment to understand what he's getting at.

'It's both of ours,' I tell him. 'We're sharing.'

He drops his head low and groans in despair, as if he can't quite believe that I've brought this latest indignity to his door. He sounds like he's in actual pain.

'For fuck's sake, Emmet,' I say, raising my voice and allowing myself to grow crankier now that our flights are behind us. 'It's just for one night. What does it matter? We're going to be fast asleep in a few hours anyway.'

'I don't like sharing rooms.'

'You share a room with Damian all the time.'

'That's different. He's my friend.'

'Well, feel free to go downstairs and book a separate one for yourself if you have a spare €400 in your wallet. But if you don't, then pick left or right and maybe lay off the complaining for five minutes, all right? Cos I'm tired, jetlagged, and have had enough of it.'

He opens his eyes wide in surprise. This is the first time I've displayed any annoyance since shaking him awake in

North Bondi some twenty-seven hours ago, and perhaps he's realized that he's lost any power he had over me now that we've finally arrived on the other side of the world. The truth is, I haven't the energy for any more of this behaviour. It doesn't help that the closer we get to the island, the more anxious I'm growing over whether this has been a good idea or not. Particularly as there's still something I haven't told him.

We each take a shower and, while I emerge in a towel, planning on changing in the room, he takes his fresh clothes with him into the bathroom so he can dress in there when he's finished. It displays a curious need for modesty considering I see him in his swimmers on the beach on a regular basis. But it's different circumstances, I suppose. Lying on my bed, idly scrolling through my emails, I notice his phone charging by the side table and, hearing the sound of running water, I can't help myself. I reach for it and go straight to his photos. None of the recent pictures are in any way incriminating, although, to my surprise, he's taken a photo of me while I was asleep on the Sydney–Dubai leg, where I look rather at peace, a half-smile on my face at whatever dream I was having. Moving to his messages, I can see this same picture has been forwarded to Damian, only edited so a drawing of a penis emerges from my forehead, which in turn has led to a series of nonsensical emojis from his friend. Despite myself, I laugh.

When he reappears, fully dressed, his hair wet, I suggest a walk around the city, and he looks at me as if I've proposed that we go salsa dancing. I read this as my cue that it would be in both our interests to spend a little time apart, so tell him that, regardless, I'm going out to explore, will probably find somewhere for a meal later and will text to see whether he wants to join me.

'So you won't be coming back here first?' he asks, and I shake my head, happy to leave him in peace.

'No. And if you'd prefer to just stay in and order room service, that's fine too. I mean, it'd be a shame to miss out on seeing some of Dublin, but if you need some alone time—'

'I do,' he replies quickly.

'OK,' I say, knowing exactly how he feels.

'I'm sorry about earlier,' he adds as I reach for my jacket, perhaps feeling an impulse towards harmony now that he knows he won't have to be in my company for a while. 'In Dubai, I mean. I was just tired. And a bit nervous.'

'It's OK,' I say, not wishing to revisit that moment. 'I'll see you later.'

As I leave, I notice a Do Not Disturb sign hanging on the inside of the door and pick it up.

'Shall I put this outside?' I ask, and he nods.

'Thanks.'

Although Rebecca was born in Dublin, and lived there until moving to England in her early twenties, I've never been to Ireland before and wander the city centre, glancing idly in the windows of shops, before entering a bookshop, thinking I could probably do with buying a couple more thrillers to get me through the days ahead and the eventual flight home. The gods are clearly intent on tormenting me, however, because as I step inside, I'm confronted by a tower of Furia's novel on the New Releases table. It's piled high – it really is turning into a global phenomenon – with a sticker on the front proclaiming that it's 'soon to be a major motion picture', as opposed, I assume, to a minor one.

Unlike the edition I saw in Sydney Airport, this one is resplendent in hard covers and bears a different jacket. As I study it, a young woman pushes a trolley laden with books towards the next table.

'Have you read that?' she asks, and I shake my head. 'We can't keep it in stock.'

I glance down. There must be thirty copies here at least, so clearly they can.

'What's it about?' I ask.

Of course I know exactly what it's about, but I'm interested to know how she'll describe it. I remember Furia once telling me of a creative writing tutor who had asked this question of his students about the books they were writing, but insisted that they reference neither the plot nor the characters in their reply. She turns her head in the direction of a staircase, giving my question some thought.

'I think it's about selfishness,' she says finally, then nods, apparently satisfied by her response.

'It's a love story, I assume?'

'Why would you think that?' she asks. 'Because it's written by a woman?'

'No, because most novels are.'

'Do you really think so?'

'I do,' I say. 'Art is generally about love, one way or another, don't you think? Every book. Every song. Every film. All of us trying to live with it. Or get over it. Or wonder why we've never had it. Not necessarily love in a sexual sense. Love between parents and children. Love for a place.'

She remains silent, considering this. Her expression suggests she'd like to contradict me but can't quite decide how.

'Who's the selfish one anyway?' I ask. 'In the book, I mean.'

'They all are,' she replies. 'The main characters – she's a drover, which is—'

'I know what a drover is.'

'You're Australian?' she asks, and I nod. I might not have been born there, but I have permanent residency, after all, so I consider myself a native now. 'I can hear it in your accent,' she tells me. 'Anyway, she breaks up a marriage. Although it was an unhappy marriage.'

'And that makes it OK?'

'Well, it's more complicated than that. There are three people at the heart of the story, and they hurt each other at every turn. But they've all been hurt themselves in the past so, somehow, we forgive them. In the end, the reader just wants everyone to survive and be happy. And of course there's the unreliable narrator, which is what everyone talks about.'

'And do they?' I ask.

'Do they what?'

'Survive.'

'That would be giving it away.'

'I just want to know if things work out for them,' I say. 'A writer once told me that was the reason she wrote fiction. To give people happy endings.'

'Sorry, no spoilers,' she tells me. 'You'll have to finish it to find out.'

I arrive back at the hotel much later than intended, check on Emmet, who's in a deep sleep, before going down to the bar, sitting with Furia's book before me, unable to open it. I drink more than I should – perhaps my body is out of sync after the last couple of days – before eventually making my way a little unsteadily towards the lift. I suspect that, tomorrow morning, I might regret not having gone straight to bed.

It's been many years since I've slept in the same bedroom as my son, and I find his presence strangely comforting. He's sleeping in a T-shirt and boxer shorts, his right arm slung over the side of the bed, his left leg sticking out from beneath the duvet. Part of me feels slightly disconcerted by how beautiful I find him. There were moments in his childhood when I found him so utterly perfect that it was difficult not to weep when he came running towards me. When I would bring him to Nippers, I would study his small body and fear that I was fetishizing his splendour. I wanted him to stay that way for ever, never to change. And it seems as if it's only now, in moments of repose, when he's not being a pain-in-the-ass teen, that his childhood flawlessness is momentarily restored.

I suppose I looked like him once, long ago, too. Utterly innocent.

Maybe that's why Freya chose me.

It's just gone noon when we check out and, happily, Emmet has woken in good spirits, while I, on the other hand, feel a little rough. He seems almost excited when we board the train at Heuston Station, heading in the direction of Galway.

'Don't,' he says when he sees me smiling.

'Don't what?' I ask.

'You're thinking about my trains,' he says, and I laugh, despite myself.

'Yes,' I admit. 'Those bloody things.'

At the age of five, only a year after Rebecca left, Emmet became obsessed with toy trains, constructing an elaborate system of railway lines that ran around our home, carriages, signals, tiny buildings and miniature figures everywhere. Every birthday and Christmas, it was the only thing he wanted. It was a harmless hobby, although I had to make my peace with how much of the apartment they took over. And then, one day, about three years ago, I came home to find his entire collection disassembled, boxed up and placed for sale on eBay. He sold it to a collector for a surprisingly large amount and I found myself missing them afterwards. For all my professional training, it took a while for me to recognize that their loss signalled the end of a special period in our lives. When I suggested this to him a few weeks later, he buried his head in his hands and pleaded with me, for the thousandth time, not to psychoanalyse him.

'Here's the difference between you and me, Dad,' he said. 'You see me selling them as a sign that I'm getting older, which means you're getting older, so you're thinking about your mortality and the fact that, one day, you'll die. While, for me, it's much less complicated. I just want a better board and a couple of hundred dollars in my bank account for the summer.'

'Wow,' I said as I tried to take this in.

'And I didn't even have to spend seven years in medical school to figure that out,' he added with a grin.

It was hard to argue with that assessment.

Now, as this real-life train makes its way across the country, through Kildare, Tullamore and Athlone, we're at ease with each other, chatting about inconsequential matters. Only as we pass through Ballinasloe, with less than an hour to go, do I dare to ask how's he feeling now about seeing his mother.

'Fine,' he says, non-committally.

'Your enthusiasm is overwhelming.'

'Whatever.'

'Don't *whatever* me,' I say. 'It's complicated being a parent.'

'Sure.'

I can see from the expression on his face that his anger with Rebecca is what's making him try to provoke me. It crosses my mind that he'll probably be a father himself one day and, when that happens, he'll be good at it. Each year as he's advanced through the Nippers colours, from red to brown, he's shown himself to be particularly concerned with looking after younger children, encouraging them, watching out for their safety in the waves and lending them a helping hand whenever needed. It's one of the things that makes me think his idea of becoming a lifeguard is a good one.

It was only six months ago, during that conversation, that I told him about his Aunt Emma, who drowned off a Wexford beach when Rebecca and her parents were holidaying there decades earlier. He was shocked by this revelation – he'd never even known that she existed – and I could see that it left a deep impression on him. Later that day, he phoned his mother to ask about her and she refused to engage in the conversation, insisting that Emmet return the phone to me, when she read me the riot act.

'He's our son,' I told her. 'He had to know sometime.'

'You didn't tell him anything else, did you? About why she did it?'

'Of course not.'

'Do you think I should?' she asked, her tone softening.

'Well, not over the phone.'

'Obviously not.'

'But maybe next time you see him?'

There was a lengthy silence.

'I don't want to bring that darkness into his life,' she said. 'You haven't brought yours into his either.'

'Maybe he needs to hear it,' I suggested. 'So he can understand both of us better. He's not a child any more.'

As I'm recalling this, out of the blue, Emmet says, 'Dad, there's something I need to tell you.'

'Go on,' I say, snapping back to the moment.

'It's about yesterday evening.'

'What about it?'

'When you left me alone in the hotel.'

My mind spins in a dozen different directions. I know I was gone far longer than expected – and, in the end, I never bothered to text him, assuming he would contact me if he wanted to meet – but surely nothing untoward could have taken place during my few hours of absence.

'What about it?' I ask nervously.

'It's just . . .' He hesitates and takes a deep breath. 'The thing is—'

'What? Just spit it out.'

'I nearly . . .'

I'm ready to shake him now to get whatever it is out of him.

'Nearly what? Just tell me.'

He looks out the window, shakes his head, then turns back, looking down at the table that separates us and scratching it awkwardly with his thumb.

'I nearly had a threesome.'

I'm not certain that I've heard him right. How is that even possible? He knows absolutely no one in Dublin. And he's only fourteen. The same age I was when—

'All I needed,' he adds, 'was two other people.'

There's a few moments of silence before he bursts out laughing, collapsing back in the seat, his knees pressed up against his chest. It takes me a minute to get the joke and, when I do, I can't quite believe that he'd prank me like this, but I find myself laughing too, unable to stop. Tears roll down both our faces and some of the other passengers turn to look at us in irritation. I would like to preserve this moment for ever. The two of us, on this train, heading towards Galway, laughing over the silliest joke I've ever heard in my life.

'God, I miss the beach,' he says a little later, looking out as the green fields pass us by. 'My body literally feels like it's drying out.'

'I miss it too, actually.'

'I will never live anywhere but Sydney.'

I expect to feel pleased by this declaration but, as much as I want to keep him close, I also want him to explore the world, something that I've failed to do in my life so far. A thought occurs to me that I still could. No matter what Emmet says, I'm not Jurassic. I'm only forty. So I'll be forty-four if and when he goes to uni. That's still young.

'There are beaches in other countries,' I tell him. 'I'm pretty sure the oceans stretch around the planet.'

'Long term, I mean,' he replies. 'When I'm really old and settling down. Like, twenty-seven or whatever.'

I stifle a laugh.

'Well, at least we're going to an island,' I tell him. 'You can probably swim there.'

'Can I ask you something?' he says.

'Sure.'

'Furia.'

'What about her?'

'Do you think . . .' He pauses and bites his lip as if he

wants to ensure that he phrases this exactly right. 'Do you think that if you'd never met her, then you and Mum would still be together? And that she wouldn't have abandoned me?'

I've never heard him use this particular word before to describe his estrangement from Rebecca. Would he prefer to lay all culpability for his parents' break-up at Furia's feet? I can't say that I blame him, but I don't want to lie to him either. It would be unfair to both of them, and to him too.

But it's not the time to answer.

'Can we have this conversation another time?' I ask him. 'It's a long story, and we're too close to Galway. But I will talk about it with you, I promise.'

He sighs, then nods his head, before taking his Air-Pods out, putting them in his ears, and looking out the window. I silently curse myself. I've fucked up again.

10

NEITHER REBECCA NOR I had ever been to Australia
but, two years after we married, she was offered
the opportunity to complete her training in Sydney and
we made the decision to relocate.

Although it stretched our budget, we chose to rent an
apartment on Waruda Street in Kirribilli for a few months
while we got to know the city. Our balcony faced directly
on to the Opera House and there were mornings, as we
breakfasted, when I felt an overwhelming sense of well-
being, an inner peace that I hadn't experienced in a long
time. One night, drunk, we even had sex – a rare treat –
and, as fate would have it, that was the night Emmet was
conceived.

Rebecca reacted to her pregnancy better than I expected,
given her previous determination not to bring a child
into the world, and we might have gone on like that for
ever, two companionable people in a sexless relationship,
bringing up their son, had Furia Flyte not entered our
lives.

We first met at a birthday party when Emmet was three.
We had quite a small circle of friends, as Rebecca's schedule once she was qualified left little time for socializing,

and I was alone with him much of the time. I formed good relationships with the parents who helped out at Nippers, growing friendly with another set of parents, Belinda and Jake, a full-time lifeguard who proposed to teach me surfing. Their son, Damian, had bonded with Emmet on their first day in Kindy and the two boys had rarely lost sight of each other since.

Eventually, it seemed sensible that we should all meet, and we began with a Saturday-lunchtime date in the Ravesis, a lively spot that afforded views of the surfers making their way towards the beach. Somewhat to my surprise, Rebecca and Belinda hit it off, and I saw a side to my wife that I hadn't often observed before. Carefree, relaxed, unencumbered by the past. She liked Jake too and a comfortable friendship developed, pushed along by our sons' growing bond.

Jake's thirtieth-birthday party took place in a nightclub in Bondi. Having lived in Sydney for a few years by now, I was accustomed to beautiful people. Hardly a day went by when my head wasn't turned by the women who passed me on the street. But in my life I had never laid eyes on anyone as beautiful as the woman I met there. I'd never even imagined that such women existed.

When I first saw her, she was standing alone by a trestle table, sipping from a glass of champagne and looking out towards the sea. Her skin was a dark ebony, her hair shaved close to the skull, allowing her extraordinary bone sculpting to come to the fore. Rebecca had vanished into the crowd, and I found myself gravitating towards her.

She looked at me rather coolly as I advanced and I guessed that she was not unaccustomed to men approaching her, but, after all, we were at a private party, which meant that we must both have some connection to the hosts.

'Can I join you?' I asked.

She nodded and we fell into conversation easily. When she threw her head back and laughed at some remark I made about the latest government crisis, I felt a premonition, and a strong desire, that this would prove more than just a random encounter.

We exchanged details about our lives. I told her about my job, and she confessed that, while she currently worked in a theatre, she had aspirations towards being a writer. Possibly a playwright. Possibly a novelist. Possibly a screenwriter. Possibly all three. She'd published some short stories, she told me, including one in an American anthology, and had had a one-act play produced at the previous year's Sydney Festival. She betrayed neither narcissism nor false humility as she talked about her ambitions, admitting that she'd already written a novel that had been rejected by publishers.

'Fuckers,' I said.

'No, it wasn't good enough. They were right to turn it down.'

'And you're working on something else?'

'Always.'

'Will this be the one?'

'I'm twenty-nine,' she told me with a shrug. 'And my plan was always to get published before I turn thirty, so that ship's probably sailed. But there's nothing else that I want to do with my life than tell stories.'

'Why?' I asked.

'Because unlike in the real world, when a writer invents characters, we get to decide how their stories end. Happy or sad.'

'And which do you favour?'

'Oh, happy,' she told me without hesitation. 'Always happy. Readers need to feel that there's hope.'

'For the characters?'

'No. For them.'

I felt a deep desire to tell her how beautiful she was but restrained myself. But it wasn't just her face or her body to which I was attracted. It was deeper than that. I wanted to know her in every way that you can know a person.

'I haven't even asked your name,' I said when we were on our second glass of champagne.

'Furia,' she said, extending a hand. 'Furia Flyte.'

'Sounds like a pen name.'

'I know. But I swear it's real. And you?'

'Aaron Umber.'

'Your accent,' she said. 'You're not from here, are you?'

'No,' I said, telling her a little about the city where I'd grown up.

'I haven't travelled much yet. Although I'd like to.'

I'd almost forgotten that I was at a party. It seemed like we were just two people who'd met in a club and been drawn to each other. I couldn't be certain that the attraction was mutual, but I felt it was.

After we'd been talking for around forty minutes, Rebecca joined us, introducing herself to Furia, who looked at me with a disenchanted expression on her face, as if she was both surprised and unsurprised that I had failed to mention the existence of a wife. The conversation became stilted then, and I looked over the balcony towards the waves crashing on to the shore, feeling a desperate urge to throw myself into the water and swim out as far as I could.

It was Rebecca, however, who brought Furia back into our lives a few weeks later. We had a spare ticket to a concert, and she suggested offering it to her.

'Why?' I asked. 'We barely know her.'

'Actually, I had a coffee with her on Tuesday.'

I was startled by this admission, and immediately envious, having spent a lot of time since Jake's party trying to contrive a reason to meet again while my wife had simply done the sensible thing and phoned her up.

'Why did you do that?' I asked.

'Because we got along and exchanged numbers,' she replied with a shrug, as if it was the most obvious thing in the world. 'Why, didn't you like her?'

'She seemed fine,' I said.

'I mean, we don't have to,' she told me. 'We can invite someone else if you prefer.'

'No, it's fine,' I replied. 'It would be nice to see her again.'

Furia replied to Rebecca's text invitation with a *yes*, and I spent the days leading up to the gig obsessing over what I would wear.

'Have you done something with your hair?' Furia asked when we found a small bar for drinks after the show had ended.

'He's had it styled,' said Rebecca, a mocking note creeping into her tone. 'He usually just gets it cut, but this afternoon, he had it styled apparently.'

'It looks good,' she replied, her eyes meeting mine.

'Thank you,' I said.

'You haven't added highlights, have you?'

'Christ no,' I told her. 'I'm not some ageing boyband member. I'm naturally blond but it lightens even more during the summer.'

Standard conversation followed, questions about Emmet, asking how Rebecca and I had first met, and soon, the subject of whether she was seeing anyone arose. My heart beat a little faster in my chest as I waited for her reply.

'Not right now,' she said. 'I think I've sworn off men.'

'Really?' asked Rebecca. 'Why?'

'Cos I'm fucking sick of them. Every guy I've been with has done something to let me down. I just think I've reached the point where I'm wondering whether I need the hassle. They're either using apps on the side, looking for nothing more than a shag, or they're married. Or all three. The truth is, we only really need a man in order to have a child. And even then, they're pretty much disposable afterwards.'

'None taken,' I said, and she smiled.

'I think I just need to mix it up a bit,' she continued, looking around the bar as if she hoped the right man might be sitting somewhere nearby just waiting to introduce himself. 'No more fuckboys. I need to try someone different to my usual type.'

'Like who?' I asked, ready to transform myself into whatever that might be.

'I haven't figured that out yet. Not an Aussie, that's for sure. Someone with experience of life outside Sydney. One of the benefits of writing, if I ever get published, that is, will be the opportunities I'll have to see the world. Maybe I'll meet someone amazing in, you know, Argentina or Denmark or someplace like that.'

'Of course you'll get published,' I said.

'How do you know? You haven't read anything I've written.'

'I offered.'

'No, you didn't,' she said, and she was right; I had merely thought it on the night we met but considered it too forward to ask.

'Well, I'm offering now,' I said. 'I'd love to read your work.'

'Aaron,' said Rebecca, 'all you ever read is thrillers.'

'Then it would be good to broaden my horizons, wouldn't it? Obviously I wouldn't be able to give you any great critique but, I mean, if you'd like a reader, then . . . I know it's a very personal thing . . .' I let the sentence drift away, conscious that I might be sounding a little ridiculous.

'Well, thank you,' said Furia, reaching over and placing a hand atop my own and squeezing it. 'That's kind of you. Let me think about it.'

I ordered more drinks and went to the bathroom, looking myself in the mirror and throwing some water on my face. Although I was only in my twenties, so was still a young man, I couldn't help but think that this is how it must feel to be young, an experience that seemed to have passed me by. The only real difference, after all, between me and a fifteen-year-old virgin going on his first date was that when a kid that age was trying to impress a girl, he didn't usually have his wife sitting between them.

When I returned to the table, Furia and Rebecca were locked in conversation and, for a time, it felt as if they weren't even aware of my presence.

'Have you been on a plane that Rebecca has flown?' asked Furia, turning to me eventually, and I shook my head.

'Not yet, no,' I said. 'When she's away, I'm home with Emmet.'

'And would you trust her?'

'Well, she's a terrible driver,' I said. 'So I'm not sure.'

'No, I'm not,' said Rebecca, frowning.

'You are.'

'You've never said that before.'

'Sparing your feelings.'

'I'm a perfectly safe driver,' she insisted, turning to Furia.

'Try being her passenger.'

'I don't know why you're saying this. It's simply not true.'

'Relax,' I told her. 'I'm just teasing.'

'Well, stop. I don't like it.'

There's nothing more uncomfortable than couples arguing in public, so I bit my tongue, particularly as I couldn't quite understand why I was saying something that was actually completely untrue. The evening ended soon after and, true to form, Rebecca and I, on the verge of a row, went to bed without exchanging another word.

A week later, I contrived to be near the University of Sydney and met Furia as she was coming out of a seminar. I pretended that this was a chance encounter before inviting her for a drink. We went to a bar in Redfern where the sun bore down as we sat beneath canopies in a beer garden, sunglasses on so we didn't have to read each other's eyes. We talked for a long time, quite intimately, and then:

'Can I ask, what happened to you?' she asked me in a cautious, gentle tone.

'How do you mean?'

'You have a . . .' She thought about it, searching for the right phrase. 'You have a sadness inside you, Aaron. I saw it the night we met at Jake's birthday party. And – I don't mean to be rude, it's not a criticism – but an emotional immaturity. You look younger than your years too, which is odd. It's like you're stunted in some way.'

The phrase hit home. I was still the awkward boy approaching Freya after she explained the benefits of a career in medicine to my school group, telling me that if I was interested in learning more about her profession, then she had some introductory textbooks in her apartment that she could loan me, and I could come home with her and borrow them.

'Something happened to me,' I told her carefully. 'Years ago now. I was just a kid at the time.'

'Something sexual, I assume?'

'Yes.'

'At the hands of a man?'

'No, a woman.'

She sat back and nodded, considering this.

'That's unusual,' she said.

'It's actually more common than you might imagine. No one talks about it, except to joke about it.'

'Do you want to tell me more?'

I shook my head. 'Another time, perhaps. When we get to know each other better.'

'Isn't this exactly how we get to know each other better?' she asked. 'By talking about things like this?'

'Honestly, it's too sad a story. And this is too beautiful a day. I'd prefer to just sit here with you and not sing any sad songs.'

'Tell me about Rebecca, then.'

'What would you like to know?'

'Are you happy with her?'

My vacillation probably said it all. I simply couldn't think of a truthful answer to the question.

'She's very beautiful,' she said eventually.

'She is,' I agreed.

'And smart.'

'Yes. But—'

'But what?'

'I don't want to frighten you away by saying something too intimate.'

'I don't mean to pry. Don't say anything that makes you uncomfortable.'

'She doesn't love me,' I said immediately, expressing something aloud that I had always known but never had the courage to admit aloud. 'And I don't think she ever has. I don't think she knows what love is.'

'Men always say things like that,' she said, sighing, and I worried that I was disappointing her by sounding like a cliché. 'It's always the woman's fault.'

'No, I didn't mean—'

'It's OK.'

She turned away. A young couple was walking down the street hand in hand, the reverse of us in that the boy was black and the girl was white, he with his head thrown back in laughter at something she was saying.

'Why would you say such a thing about your own wife?' she asked.

'Too,' I said.

'Too? I don't understand.'

'I say *I love you*, but she says *I love you too*. It's never the other way around. She never initiates it.'

'Perhaps she thinks it goes unsaid.'

'It should never go unsaid.'

'Do you still sleep together?'

'That's all we do,' I told her, laughing bitterly. 'Sleep together. Physical intimacy has never been much of a thing between us.'

'How come? You're hot. She's hot.'

I felt thrilled by the compliment.

'She makes me feel worthless,' I continued, uncertain why I was opening up like this. Did I want her to pity me? To take me home to her apartment and fuck me? 'Ugly. Unattractive. Unworthy. I'm still a young man, Freya. I want someone to look at me and want me. Why shouldn't I have that? Others do. You must get it all the time. Why shouldn't I have that? What's wrong with me?'

'Furia,' she said.

'What?'

'You called me Freya.'

'No, I didn't.'

'You did.'

Trying to read her mind, I wondered whether she was looking into the future, at what might happen between us in a week, a month, a year, ten years, if this connection grew deeper and she became the catalyst for the end of my marriage. Whether she was imagining what it might be like to be naked with me, as I was imagining what it might be like to be naked with her. I stretched my arm out, leaving a hand on the table, hoping that she would give me some signal, place hers atop mine as she had after the concert. She seemed to be considering it because she stared at it for a long time before deciding against. Perhaps, when Rebecca had been present, it had felt like an inconsequential act, whereas here, with just the two of us present, it would take on greater significance. Or perhaps it was because it was my left hand, and my wedding ring was visible on my fourth finger.

'Be honest with me, Aaron,' she said. 'Because whatever is going to happen next depends on the answer to this question. Do you believe that you and Rebecca have a future together? Do you want one?'

I took a long time to answer. I could physically feel my heart beating in my chest. The fact that she was even considering being with me made me hard. But I couldn't answer. I failed in this crucial moment and, after a minute or two of silence, she looked away, raised a hand to the waiter and asked for the bill. As usual, I simply didn't know how to behave.

As we left, however, I took hold of her arm and asked her why she had asked me that question. She took off her sunglasses and looked directly at me.

'Because I don't want to be responsible for breaking up a marriage if there's a chance it can survive. Or if it should survive.'

I took a chance.

'It can't. It won't,' I told her. 'You want to know something? The night before we got married, Rebecca's mother said something to me that I've never forgotten.'

'What was it?'

'She said, don't marry her. You're a fool if you do.'

'Her own mother said that?'

I nodded.

'Wow,' she replied. 'That explains a lot.'

'Does it?' I asked. 'What does it explain?'

She shook her head and said that we'd talked enough for one day, that she had some thinking to do and, before I could remonstrate with her and ask could we move on somewhere else, a taxi passed, she raised her hand, hailed it, and was gone.

We didn't see each other for some weeks after that but began exchanging text messages. These were not casual messages but were almost always about the status of Rebecca's and my relationship. Whether we were getting on better, spending time together, having sex. I began to worry that Furia was using me, or us, as research for a novel she was writing, but I didn't want to challenge her in case it led to her cutting me off.

What's happening with us? I asked in one late-night text, and although I could see that she had read it immediately, it took her more than an hour to reply.

I'm worried that I'm going to hurt you, she replied eventually. *And you've been hurt enough already.*

I'm willing to risk it.

Finally, one night, racked with desire, I showed up at her apartment building, pressing the buzzer to tell her that I was downstairs. Rather than inviting me up, however, she took the lift down to the lobby, looking both angry at my intrusion and also rather anxious.

'You can't just show up here like this,' she told me.

'I needed to see you.'

She glanced around, and a thought – a terrible thought – occurred to me.

'Do you have someone upstairs?' I asked. She shook her head, but I could tell that she was lying and felt almost sick with jealousy. 'You do, don't you?'

'Fine. I do. I have a life, you know. And I don't answer to you.'

'So much for having sworn off men. You never said there was anyone else in the picture,' I said, furious with myself to hear the obvious emotion in my voice.

'You never asked. I don't know if you realize it, Aaron, but all we ever talk about is you. Your life. Your marriage. Your son. Your career. Your past. Your pain. We never talk about me at all. You never ask.'

'That's not true,' I insisted, surprised that this was how she saw me.

'It is,' she insisted. 'You tell me all the things that are wrong with your relationship, but you never talk to Rebecca about it. You speak to me like I'm your therapist.'

'I speak to you like someone I'm in love with.'

She reared back at this, looking shocked, which astonished me. She couldn't possibly have been surprised by this.

'Aaron, you barely know me.'

'But I want to. I mean it. I'm in love with you.'

'Oh, for God's sake.'

'You're all I think about.'

She shook her head, looking pissed off, which, in turn, pissed me off.

'Are you writing about me?' I asked angrily. 'About us? Is that what this has all been about?'

'No,' she said, wrapping her arms around her body defensively.

'Then just tell me. I don't understand what it is that you want from me.'

'I don't want anything.'

'Then what has all this been about?'

'All of what?' she asked, raising her voice angrily.

'This,' I said in exasperation, looking around as if the lobby of her building was the ground floor of our private home. 'Everything that we've built between us.'

'We've built nothing between us, Aaron. I told you early on that I'm not interested in men any more. That I'm sick to death of men and their fucking bullshit. Bullshit like this. I want something different.'

'Then why do we meet? Why do we text? You say all I ever talk about is me and the state of my marriage, but that's all you seem to be interested in, as if you've been trying to decide whether or not you should be the person who comes between Rebecca and me.'

'That is what I've been trying to decide,' she said.

'I don't understand,' I said, utterly baffled, because she seemed to be contradicting herself at every turn.

'I've spent a lot of time thinking about this. And I've realized that I should. You're not right for each other. You're not. You'll never make each other happy. And you're both too young to be living such loveless lives. You both need more.'

'So you are interested, then?' I asked.

'In what?'

'In me.'

She buried her head in her hands and groaned loudly before looking back at me.

'No, Aaron, I'm not. For one thing, you've lied to me.'

I took a step back, a chill spreading across my body.

'What have I lied about?'

'Do I need to spell it out?'

I stared at her. I knew what she was referring to but couldn't bring myself to admit it. And my mind was spinning as I tried to understand how she could possibly know.

'You're a kind man, Aaron,' she continued. 'A decent man. And I have nothing but sympathy for what you've been through. But I'm not interested in you in a romantic sense and that's never going to change. The truth is, I'm in love with someone else.'

I felt as if I was about to stop breathing.

'So all of this has been for nothing?' I asked. 'You've just been leading me on?'

'I've been leading you absolutely nowhere. You've just been walking behind me all this time, trying to keep up, and haven't seen what's been staring you in the face.'

Before I could say anything more, the bell above the lift sounded and the doors opened. Emerging barefoot, wearing only a pair of denim shorts and a T-shirt, a figure emerged, looking from me to Furia and back again.

My brain couldn't immediately comprehend how this person was here. Or why. It simply didn't make any sense.

Furia turned around, saw her, and looked down at the floor.

'I'm sorry,' said Rebecca, looking almost relieved that the truth had finally been revealed. 'This wasn't how either of us wanted you to find out.'

II

A MAN NAMED CIAN Ó'Droighneáin picks us up from Galway harbour in a small boat and tells us that it won't take more than an hour to reach the island. I see Emmet visibly spring to life, like a wilting flower, when he's close to water again. Somehow, the waves of the Atlantic Ocean look and smell different to those that lap towards Bondi, Manly, Coogee, or any of the other beaches I'm familiar with from Sydney. Even as the spray splashes across my face, it tastes different on my tongue. Darker, more threatening, offering a warning that travellers pass through its current at their own risk. I wonder how many souls it has claimed over the centuries in revenge for intrusion. For Emmet, however, who lets his right hand rest within it, it's a return to his comfort zone after the lengthy plane and train journeys, as if he has reverted to the warmth and sanctuary of the womb.

The Bish. Half boy / half fish.

Before leaving Sydney, I located a small cottage online and booked it for three nights. A taxi driver waiting by the port drives us up a winding road towards it, depositing us with little ceremony by the front door. The owner of the lodging, one Peader Dooley, has emailed to say that I will find a key beneath a plant pot by the front door, and he is true to his word. Stepping inside, I'm struck by the musty smell and I suspect it hasn't been occupied in some time. Opening the windows, I turn the light on – a single bare bulb hanging from the ceiling – and look around, surveying the room, which is either a kitchen that houses a living room or a living room that houses a kitchen. It's hard to tell. Emmet, frowning, is focused entirely on his phone.

'There's no Wi-Fi,' he says, his tone one of utter disbelief. 'Dad, there's no Wi-Fi,' he repeats, louder now.

'Should I call the police?' I ask, and he stares at me for a moment, as if he thinks I'm genuinely suggesting this, before rolling his eyes. 'We're in a fairly isolated place, Emmet,' I tell him. 'It's possible there won't be any Wi-Fi on the island at all.'

'None?'

'I mean, it's possible.'

'How do they survive?'

It does seem a little disconcerting to be so removed from the outside world – even I'm willing to admit that – but it wasn't as if I had many options. There were no hotels and this was the only cottage available. I leave him to make his peace with digital isolation and take a look in the bedroom, where I'm greeted by a single bed. Before Emmet can notice it and start screaming like a banshee, I tell him that I'll sleep on the sofa and allow him his privacy.

'Do people actually live here?' he asks, sounding amazed, as if he's just walked on to the set of a historical movie.

'Well, it's a rental,' I tell him. 'So probably not all year round.'

'But what about the other houses?'

'I don't know,' I say with a shrug. 'They're probably a bit more up to date.'

He starts taking photos on his phone and I know he wants to send them to Damian or one of his other friends with some sarcastic comment attached but then realizes that, without Wi-Fi, to do so would cost him a small fortune.

'Look, we'll make the most of it,' I say cheerfully. 'Communing with nature and all that.'

He opens his mouth to protest but recognizes that this is exactly the sort of sentiment that he would generally endorse, so remains silent.

'Right,' I add, assuming that we're done with the complaints for now. 'Do you want to wash up or shall we just head straight out?'

'Where are we meeting her?' he asks.

'Who?'

'Mum.'

'Ah,' I reply, realizing that I can't delay this revelation any longer. I've been putting off telling him, but it really can't wait. 'You might want to take a seat.'

He does as instructed, collapsing into a threadbare armchair that, even from where I'm standing, has a faint feline scent to it, looking a little anxious.

'Go on,' he says.

'The thing is, I probably should have mentioned this before, but your mother doesn't actually know we're coming.'

There's a lengthy pause while he takes this in.

'I'm sorry,' he asks, shaking his head as if he can't quite
make sense of my words. 'What?'

'She doesn't . . . I didn't tell her.'

'What do you mean, you didn't tell her?'

'I don't really know how else to put it.'

'But how could you . . . why not?'

'Well, it's not as if we talk that often.'

'No, but . . .' He raises his voice and throws his arms in
the air. 'She invited us, didn't she?'

'Not in so many words. When she phoned to tell me
the news, she simply said that she was coming here for
the funeral and to let you know that your grandmother
had died. She didn't actually say that we should travel
over for it.'

Emmet's eyes open wide.

'Dad,' he says, trying to control his emotions. 'We've
flown halfway across the world! What if she's not even
here?'

'Of course she'll be here,' I tell him. 'The funeral is
tomorrow, after all. Where else would she be?'

He shakes his head, trying to make sense of this.

'So she didn't want us to come?' he asks, more of a
whisper now.

'It's not so much that she didn't want us to come,' I
explain. 'It's more that she didn't specifically say that we
should.'

'What if she's angry?'

'She won't be.'

He shakes his head, unconvinced, and looks around
in despair.

'This is insane,' he says, as much to himself as to me. 'I should have been taken into care years ago. You're both nuts. You're both completely fucking nuts.'

I stifle a laugh. He doesn't sound so much angry as perplexed, but, to my relief, he's not responding to the news as badly as I feared he would. I make my way over to the sink and turn the tap on. The water runs a hideous brown for the best part of a minute before turning clear. I pour a glass and sip it cautiously. It's cold, fresh and delicious.

'So how do we find her?' he asks, his tone exhausted but resigned.

'Well, as far as I understand it, there's only about four hundred people on the island. And a single village at the heart of it. So, I don't imagine it will be all that difficult. We could check the local pubs and, if we can't find her there, then someone will probably be able to point us in the right direction.'

'Fine,' he says. 'Either way, this will make a great story for my therapist in years to come.'

'I can probably recommend some good names if you like.'

He walks past me without even acknowledging this remark and goes into the bathroom, while I unpack our cases and leave some clean clothes out for him on his bed. I hear the shower running and decide to go outside until he's ready and look around.

It's beautiful here. Green, hilly, natural. In the distance, I hear the sound of sheep, although, looking around, I can't see any. There's a good view of the ocean and a well-worn path leading down towards it. I could imagine a person sitting outside in the sunshine, reading a book, leaving the world behind them. It's an attractive idea. Glancing to my right, I notice a raised farm on the hill next to the cottage, where a man around my age, tall and blond, is leaning on a fence, smoking a cigarette. He raises a hand in greeting and I raise mine too, considering whether I should wander over to say hello, but before I can decide he turns and disappears out of sight.

'You ready?' says a voice from behind me, and I turn to see my son, who looks refreshed, having changed into the jeans and T-shirt I laid out for him.

'Sure,' I say.

'And remember, if this goes wrong, it's on you.'

I nod, and we make our way along the path that, I assume, will lead us towards the village at the heart of the island. He turns to look in the direction of the beach and asks whether he can go swimming later, and I tell him that it might be dangerous at night, but there's no reason why he can't go down there in the morning before the funeral, and he seems satisfied by this.

'What was she like anyway?' he asks as we walk along.

'What was who like?'

'Your mother-in-law.'

'You mean your grandmother.'

'I didn't have enough of a relationship with her to call her that.'

'Nor did I. Maybe we should just call her Vanessa.'

'OK.'

'I only met her a couple of times,' I tell him. 'We went

for dinner a few nights before your mum and I got married. And then we saw a little of her during that week. After that, our paths never crossed again.'

'Why not?'

I shrug. 'Things were complicated between them. You know that.'

'Yeah, but no one's ever explained to me why. Is it just a family thing with us? Mothers who aren't interested in their kids, I mean?'

I take a breath. Perhaps now, on this brisk but sunny afternoon, in such a peaceful place, it's time to explain to him the darker aspects of Rebecca's childhood and teenage years, because God knows it's unlikely she'll ever do so herself. Maybe it will give him a better understanding of her and allow him to forgive her neglect.

'What?' he asks, when I stop for a moment and press my thumb and index finger to the corners of my eyes, trying to decide.

'If you want the answer to that question,' I tell him, 'then I'll give it to you. But it's not pretty.'

He hesitates only briefly, before nodding his head.

'I want it,' he says.

And so, as we continue to walk, I tell him the terrible story of his grandfather Brendan Carvin, and the effect his actions had, not just on the eight little girls who he raped, but on his wife and daughters too. It takes some time and I'm surprised that he listens without interruption. When I reach the end of my narrative, however, the part that sees Vanessa arrive on this island many years earlier, he stops and sways a little, like a drunken man.

'Are you all right?' I ask him.

'I need to sit down for a minute.'

And he does. Simply collapses on to the grass, as if his legs have given way beneath him. He presses his knees close to his chest and wraps his arms around them, his head buried low, as if he's trying to make himself appear as small as possible.

'Why did you never tell me any of this before?' he asks eventually, his voice so quiet that I have to struggle to hear him.

'You were too young. It's not the kind of thing you can talk about to a child.'

'My grandfather,' he says, looking up, tears forming in his eyes. 'He did things like that?'

'He wasn't your grandfather,' I tell him. 'Other than in a purely biological sense. He was just a man you never met who married a woman you never knew and fathered a daughter who gave birth to you.'

'So my grandfather.'

'You know grandfathers,' I insist. 'You know lots of your friends' grandfathers. They're different men. Good men. Kind men. Brendan Carvin was not one of them.'

'What if anyone finds out?' he asks, his voice cracking. 'My friends. People at school.' He hesitates for a moment. 'Girls.'

'No one will,' I promise. 'He's dead now.'

'Really?'

'Yes.'

'What happened to him?'

'A heart attack, I was told. So trust me, this isn't

something that anyone will ever associate you with. You don't even share a surname.'

'Did he hurt Mum?' he asks, and I shake my head.

'He didn't abuse her, if that's what you're asking. But your aunt, Emma, yes. He abused her. Repeatedly.'

'And then she drowned.'

'She took her own life,' I say.

He turns his head to the right and vomits on to the grass, quickly and violently. There's not much in his stomach to throw up and, soon, it's just dry heaves. I place my hand on his back to comfort him, but he shrugs me off and I step away, allowing him to come to terms with these revelations himself.

Time passes; a lot of time, I think. And then, finally, he rises, takes a deep breath and looks towards the centre of the island. I can read my son well. I know what he's thinking.

He wants to be with his mother.

'Let's go,' he says.

The village is even smaller than I'd imagined. A few shops. A church. And, at either end of the street, two pubs.

'Let's try here,' I say, walking towards the closer one. We step inside, where we're met with the eyes of twenty people, all of whom end their conversations immediately and turn to stare at us, like we're two naïve strangers wandering across the moors in a horror movie, unaware of the dangers we might face when night falls. I look around, taking them in, but Rebecca isn't among them. In fact, there are no women here at

all. 'Let's try the other one,' I say, but Emmet places a
hand on my arm.

'Can we just stop here for a bit?' he asks. 'I just . . . I
need to . . .'

'Of course,' I say. After everything he's just learned,
it's not unreasonable that he needs a little time to collect
his thoughts. He takes a seat at a table by the wall and the
barman walks towards us.

'What'll it be?' he asks, and, in deference to where I am,
I order a Guinness. I glance at Emmet, and he looks up.

'Make it two,' he says.

I wonder what the barman will say, hoping that his
response won't diminish my son, but he appears non-
plussed and simply nods before returning behind the bar
to pour the drinks.

'Another thing for you to tell your future therapist about,' I tell him. 'The holiday I turned you into an
alcoholic.'

'I don't think I'll be calling this a holiday,' he says.

It takes a long time for the drinks to be delivered, the
pints sitting on the counter for so long that I think the
barman might have forgotten us, but soon he tops them
off and brings them over. I take a sip of mine, relishing
the taste. I've never been much of a Guinness drinker,
but it turns out that it's true what they say: it's better in
Ireland. Emmet takes a longer draught and it's obvious
that it's taking all his willpower not to spit it out across
the table.

'People actually drink this stuff?' he asks.

'They say it's an acquired taste. I can get you a Coke if you want.'

He shakes his head and brings it to his mouth again, taking a smaller sip this time. 'When in Rome,' he adds.

We drink silently and companionably for a while, and I glance around at the pub, which is tastefully decorated and seems like the model for the kind of pre-bought Irish pubs that appear in cities around the world. Some of the patrons, I notice, are still throwing covert glances in our direction, as if they're nervous that we've brought the Plague with us.

'I get that she went through a lot of shit,' says Emmet eventually. 'Vanessa, I mean. But none of that had anything to do with me. So why did she never want to meet me?'

I let out a deep sigh. 'Honestly, I can't answer that,' I tell him. 'I liked her when I met her so I was always surprised that she didn't want to build a relationship with you. But things were so troubled between your mother and her. There was the occasional rapprochement over the years, but they never lasted very long. It always felt that any peace existed purely to be a foundation for another war.'

'It seems insane that the closest I'll ever be to her is when I'm at her funeral. And why is it here, anyway? Why did she want to be buried in this crazy place?'

'It's not a crazy place,' I say, offended on behalf of the island, to which I already feel an unexpected connection. 'I know we've only been here a few hours, but don't you think it's sort of beautiful?'

He shrugs, but I can tell that he doesn't wholly disagree.

'I can't remember the full story,' I explain. 'Rebecca explained it so long ago. But after her husband's trial, Vanessa came here – I don't know why; to recover, maybe? – but it became important to her in some way. Maybe it healed her. She'd lost a daughter, remember. And, one way or another, she'd lost a husband. The entire foundations of her life had been ripped apart. All those years of marriage. All the secrets. She told me about it herself, when we met.'

'What did she say?'

'That the first thing she did when she came here was to change her name. Remember, she'd been through a very public scandal. Her husband was well known in the media world through his associations with the Swimming Federation and the Olympics, and so on. She didn't want anyone to connect her with the things that had happened. Willow was her middle name and Hale her maiden name, so that's the name she adopted. She might have only spent a year here, but I think she considered it to be the most important of her life.'

'But no one will be able to visit the grave.'

'The islanders will.'

'And her husband? What's his name? Rick?'

'Ron. And I have no idea. You'll meet him later, I expect.'

'Did you meet him?'

'Again, very briefly.'

'And what was he like?'

'He struck me as a decent man.'

The barman passes by, throwing a few logs on the fire, and when he walks past us again, I stop him to ask whether he knows a woman named Rebecca Carvin.

'No one by that name living here,' he tells me.

'She's visiting for a few days,' I tell him. 'For a funeral.'

'Ah, that'll be Willow's funeral,' he replies, blessing himself. 'Try the old pub. End of the street. I saw them all heading that way earlier.'

'Right, thanks,' I say.

'I knew her a little,' he adds, before walking away.

'Rebecca?' I ask, surprised.

'No, Willow. She used to come in here for soup and a sandwich at lunchtime. She had a right go at me one day when I was pouring out my troubles to her. I can still see her, sitting across from me, giving me hell about what she called the endless selfishness of the middle-aged man who does what he wants and leaves his wife to pick up the pieces.' He pauses for a moment and I notice him glance at the fourth finger of his left hand, rubbing it slightly with his thumb. 'She set me straight that day, I'll tell you that. I never forgot it.'

I'm not quite sure how he expects me to respond to this but, before I can think of an answer, he has moved on. I make my way towards the bathroom and throw some water on my face, looking myself directly in the mirror, like a character in a film. When I return, I nod to my son and we stand up and leave. It's still warm outside, despite the setting sun, and as we make our way along the street, we attract more curious eyes. A teenage girl passes us and I notice how she looks at Emmet appreciatively, an unknown, handsome, tanned boy in her small community, and he offers her a small smile in return. I need it, because I'm growing increasingly nervous, my stomach churning in anxiety about the reception we'll receive when we arrive at the old pub.

When we reach the door, I pause and take a deep breath, as if I need to summon all my courage to push it open. Before I can commit to the moment, however, Emmet places a hand on my arm and I turn to look at him.

'Dad,' he says.

'Yes?'

He hesitates.

'Just to say. I know this has probably been the world's worst fortieth birthday.'

'You're not wrong there.'

'But . . .' And here he avoids my eyes, looking down at the ground beneath our feet. 'You've been a great dad.' He bites his lip, embarrassed, and says the words that I've spent my life longing to hear, a phrase without the word 'too' at the end. 'So, just to say . . . I love you. And I'm glad you brought me here.'

I tell myself not to ruin the moment by hugging him like a maniac. Instead, I simply nod and mentally record the moment, which I know I will relive many times in the future.

Then we push the door open and step inside.

This pub is filled with people, music and conversation. I look around, and it doesn't take long for me to notice a table towards the rear, where the big, burdensome body of Ron is sitting, sipping a large whiskey. He's wiping his eyes.

Next to him, dressed immaculately, her hand on his arm, is Furia.

And opposite them both, speaking animatedly, is Rebecca.

She happens to glance in my direction, then frowns, as if she doesn't quite recognize me. It's not dissimilar to my own reaction all those years ago when I discovered her in that apartment building in Sydney, her brain taking a moment to catch up with the reality before her.

It's only when our son steps out from behind me that she puts both hands to her mouth in astonishment.

She stands up slowly, leaning on the table to support herself, before making her way across the floor to greet us.

I remain where I am, allowing Emmet to approach her first.

They meet somewhere in the middle and he takes the initiative, wrapping his arms around her, hugging her close to him, and she embraces him in return.

It seems obscene, like a voyeur, to watch any further, so I turn away, but not before seeing how she has buried her face in his shoulder, her tears mixing with his.

12

ON A SMALL ISLAND like this, so isolated from the world, it surprises me that the priest who conducts the funeral service is not Irish. In fact, as I come to learn, he's Nigerian but has spent much of his life far removed from his native soil. The church, however, is almost empty. Ron, Rebecca and Furia sit in the front pew on the right-hand side of the aisle, while Emmet and I take our places on the left. Perhaps a couple of dozen island-ers are scattered in the benches behind us, but I suspect most are here simply for the Mass itself or to get out of the house. Two, however, catch my eye. The neighbour who waved to me from the farm next to the cottage earl-ier, who's dressed in a formal black suit and sits upright in his seat, occasionally brushing his blond hair out of his eyes. And a woman sitting in the very back row, who looks careworn, as if she is struggling with the very busi-ness of existence.

In his eulogy, the priest tells us that he remembers Vanessa from the time she spent here all those years ago.

'She called herself Willow Hale back then,' he says. 'And I was fortunate at the time to get to know her and to learn a little about her life. My feeling was that she was a woman both running away from and towards something. She was looking for healing and I hope that, during her exile on our island community, she found some. As many of us later discovered, she had experienced a troubled period prior to coming here but, when she left, I think her soul had been restored, at least a little. Her time in America subsequent to this was filled with joy, not least because of the happiness she found with her husband, Ron.' He offers a small nod in the direction of the man, who acknowledges it. 'But when I learned that Vanessa wanted to be buried here,' he continues, 'I will confess that the request moved me tremendously. We did not stay in touch after she left, but I can only assume that something of the serenity of this place remained with her for ever.'

He hesitates for a moment, as if he's uncertain whether he should say what he plans on saying next, glancing briefly towards the woman in the back row, as if to seek her approval. Or at least her understanding.

'Many years ago,' he continues at last, 'I found myself in London in the company of a young man who had grown up in this place and, while we had a drink together, I remarked to him that eventually, I would be buried in the earth of Nigeria, alongside my people. It was something I believed at the time, but I'm certain now that this will not come to pass. For, like Vanessa, I intend to make my final resting place here, in this peaceful paradise. Vanessa made many choices in her life, as we all do, some of which she may have regretted, but this, perhaps, was among her best.'

Afterwards, making his way around the congregation, he shakes my hand, introducing himself as Fr Ifechi Onkin.

'And you?' he asks.

'Aaron Umber,' I tell him.

'You're Australian?'

'Sort of.'

'And may I ask how you knew Vanessa?'

'Her daughter Rebecca and I were once married,' I explain. 'That boy over there, holding her hand, that's Emmet, our son.'

He looks over and takes in the scene, nodding his head.

'And were you close with your mother-in law?' he asks.

'Former mother-in-law,' I say, correcting him. 'And no. Not at all. In fact, I only met her a couple of times.'

'Well, I'm sure she appreciated your presence here.'

'No offence, Father,' I reply. 'But I'm not a religious man. I don't really believe in the afterlife. I think we get one shot at all of this, and we do our best, but when it's over, that's that. So I don't think she'll have any feelings about it one way or the other. She's gone.'

'No, you misunderstand me,' he says, reaching across, placing a hand on my arm and smiling widely. 'I wasn't referring to Vanessa. I was talking about Rebecca. It's she who will have been grateful that you travelled so far. Your marriage might not have been a success but I daresay you've cheered her immensely by choosing to be part

of today, and by ensuring that your son is present. I can
see the gratitude on her face. It offers a fine counterbal-
ance to the grief.'

Our son.

Last night, when we returned to the cottage, I felt
relieved at how well the evening had gone. Emmet had
put aside all his resentment, remaining next to his mother
throughout, even chatting amiably with Furia, who,
later, stood at the bar and had a drink with me, where I
congratulated her on the success of her novel.

'It's doing so well,' I told her. 'I see it everywhere.'

'Thank you,' she said. 'It's taken me a little by surprise,
if I'm honest.'

'A good surprise, though.'

'Of course.'

We stood there, rather self-consciously and, finally, to
break the silence, I nodded across the room towards the
woman who had once been married to me and was now
married to her.

'So how's our girl doing?' I asked tentatively, hoping
she wouldn't be offended by my choice of pronoun, but,
if anything, she seemed pleased by it, touching my arm
for a moment and squeezing it affectionately.

'All right, so far,' she said. 'You know just as well as I do
how things were between them. I don't think the mourn-
ing period will be a lengthy one, but there are issues that
remain that she still has to work through. She'll spend
years doing that, I imagine.'

'Well, she has you to help her with that. And Emmet.'

'It was so good of you to bring him.'

'It seemed like the right thing to do.'

'I told her to invite him, but she was terrified that he'd say no.'

This takes me by surprise.

'There's something I should probably let her know,' I say, pulling her away from the bar a little to a quieter spot. 'On the way here, I told him about the past. About Rebecca's father, I mean. And Emma. All of it.'

Furia breathes in deeply and considers this.

'OK,' she says.

'I don't know if it was my place or not, but in the moment it seemed right.'

We both glance over to where Rebecca and Emmet are huddled together, and it looks as if he's scrolling through photos on his phone – probably pictures of his surfing activities and his friends – and her face is bright with joy, as is his. He says something and she bursts out laughing before putting an arm around his shoulder and, for a moment, he lays his head there. Furia turns back to me.

'It was right,' she says.

Later, before going to bed, Emmet and I sat at the kitchen table together, drinking tea, and he asked a few more questions related to the revelations of earlier. It was a conversation he would have with Rebecca at some point in the future, he told me.

'You didn't say anything about it tonight, did you?' I asked, and he shook his head.

'Oh God, no. Totally not the right time.'

'It looked like you were having fun together.'

'As much as you can at a wake,' he said with a shrug. 'But I'm glad we came. And I'm glad you told me what you told me. It explains a lot of things. I mean, there's still a lot I need to understand about it, about her, about both of you, but—'

'Then there's something else,' I said.

'What? About Mum?'

'No,' I said, shaking my head. 'About me.' We'd come this far, after all. If there was ever a time to unearth all the secrets that had caused so much trauma in our lives, then this was it. And so I told him of the things that had happened to me when I was fourteen and how badly they had affected me over the years that followed. I hoped it would go some way to explaining why I could be so over-protective at times.

He listened carefully, never interrupting, and showed no sign of embarrassment throughout what was a lengthy and difficult conversation, centred around such an intimate topic. When I reached the conclusion of my tale, he looked down at the table for a long time, his brow furrowed, and neither of us spoke for quite some time. I guessed that he needed to think this through, to reframe me in his mind as someone who had gone through a childhood trauma and spent twenty-six years trying to come to terms with it. I could tell that he found nothing salacious about it but recognized what had happened for what it was. A crime.

'There's something I need to ask you,' I said finally before we said goodnight. 'I saw something, a few weeks ago, on your phone. I wasn't prying. Well, I suppose I was. But I didn't mean to. It was a stupid, thoughtless act on my part. I shouldn't have looked. But I did.'

He frowned and sat back in his chair, looking slightly alarmed.

'Some photos,' I said. 'Some photos of you.'

'My phone is full of photos of me.'

'More . . . intimate photos. Of your body.'

'Oh fuck,' he replied, putting a hand to his mouth, blushing from the base of his neck to the tips of his ears.

'I shouldn't have looked,' I repeated. 'I'm sorry. But since I did, I need to know why they were there. Who were you sending them to?'

His eyes opened wide now. 'Sending them to?' he asked. 'No one! Jesus! As if!'

'Then why did you take them?'

'Because I'm so skinny, Dad. I've been trying to build muscle. I want to keep track of my development.'

'And you needed to be naked for that?'

'It's not as if you could see my . . . anything.'

'They weren't far off.'

'But far enough!'

'You're not talking to anyone online, are you? Someone who asked for them?'

'Oh my God,' he said, burying his head in his hands. 'You are the weirdest man alive.'

'That might be true. I just don't want anyone taking advantage of you.'

'No one is. I promise.'

'You can understand why, though, right? After what I've told you about what happened to me?'

'I can,' he said. 'But still. This is really embarrassing.'

'I'm sorry.'

'Can we just never talk about it again?'

'All right,' I said. 'But you promise that you're telling me the truth?'

'I promise,' he confirmed. 'I'm a skinny fucker, that's all. And I want to bulk up. You've seen the protein shakes. And the weights. I want to build some strength, that's all.' He smiled and looked a little bashful. 'Like, I wouldn't mind, you know, having a—'

'Having a what?'

'Like, you know. A girlfriend.'

'Oh. Right,' I said. 'Of course. And you need muscles for that?'

'Well, they don't hurt. We live in Bondi, for God's sake. You've seen what the guys there are like.'

'So when I asked you on the plane about whether there was anyone you're interested in?'

'Let's just say I have a few options,' he told me, and I burst out laughing at the cheeky expression on his face.

'Lucky you.'

'I mean, if you need any tips . . .'

'Yeah, thanks,' I said. 'I'll know who to call on.'

We finished our tea and finally he yawned, saying that he was tired and should go to bed.

'But when we get back to Sydney,' he added tentatively, 'maybe we could all spend some time together. Me, you and Mum. When she's travelling through, I mean. Would that be OK?'

'Of course. I think it would be a really good idea.'

'And Furia too?'

I nodded. 'Of course. She's part of our family.'

He stood up, came around the table and leaned over, hugging me, something he hadn't done in more than a year, before walking away and closing the door to his room quietly behind him.

After the burial, when everyone else has made their way to the new pub for drinks and sandwiches, I find myself wandering around the graveyard, reading the names on the headstones and studying the dates. Some go back a hundred years or more while others are more recent.

It's a fine day, the sky is cloudless, and I feel a welcome sense of calm. The woman I'd noticed earlier in the back row is standing before one of the plots, laying flowers, and she turns to me as I approach her.

'A sad day,' she says, the standard greeting on such an occasion. 'He gave a lovely service though. Ifechi, I mean. We were lucky to get him. Lucky to keep him for so long too. He's been a good friend to me.'

I glance towards the grave that she's tending.

'My son,' she says before I can ask. 'Evan.'

'He died young,' I add, noticing that the poor boy passed away before the age of twenty-five.

'He did.'

'You must miss him.'

She nods, as if she hardly needs to express how much.

'I met Vanessa, you know,' she says. 'A long time ago now, of course. And I won't pretend that I knew her well. But I always remembered her.'

'You were on the island back then?' I ask.

'Oh, I've been stuck on this island since I was first brought here as a bride. I thought of moving away after my husband died, but I couldn't leave Evan on his own.'

I glance at the stone again and am surprised that his is the only name inscribed on the granite. *Evan Keogh*. It rings a bell somewhere in the far corners of my memory but, for now, I can't place it.

'I didn't let them put his father in here with him,' she says, guessing the question that's running through my mind. 'He's somewhere over there, in the far corner.'

She nods towards an area where the graves are far less well tended. I can't help but wonder what led her to separating the pair.

'He died young too,' she adds. 'Well, for these times, anyway. In his early sixties. Only a few weeks after Evan, as it happens.'

'What happened to him?' I asked. 'If you don't mind me asking.'

'To Charlie? Someone hit him with an axe.'

I blink, uncertain that I've heard her right.

'I'm sorry?'

'I said, someone hit him with an axe,' she repeats. 'It was quite the story at the time, although it probably wouldn't have travelled to as far away as wherever your accent is from. He had the head nearly separated from his body, would you believe. No one ever found out who did it. It was during the tourist season, so it was probably some ne'er-do-well from the mainland. Someone with a grudge against him. He'd made a few enemies in his time, had my husband.'

'So he wasn't caught?'

'You're assuming it was a man.'

'Well . . .' I begin.

'But no, whoever did it covered up their tracks very well. In the end, the Gardaí had no choice but to leave the case unsolved. It's one of life's little mysteries.'

She smiles, as if she's explaining the conclusion of a crime novel she enjoyed.

'Right,' I say. 'That must have been very upsetting for you.'

'They tried to pin it on me,' she continues. 'On account of it being our axe. But sure the only fingerprints on it were Charlie's, and he was a big man. I said it to the Gardaí at the time, I said do you think a fragile thing like me could lay a fella like him low? I wouldn't have the strength for it.'

'No,' I say, wondering whether I've run into the local lunatic. 'I imagine not.'

She takes my hand and speaks quietly. 'I'd have had to have a fierce hatred in me to build the strength for such a deed.'

I stare at her and, at last, she releases me, and her tone changes, as if none of this conversation has even taken place.

'She was kind,' she tells me then. 'Vanessa, I mean. There was a day, oh, a long time ago now, when poor Evan went missing. He was only a boy at the time, around sixteen, and the whole island thought he had drowned. She brought me a cup of tea when I was standing in the dunes, my heart sinking in fear, and, unlike all the rest of my neighbours, she wasn't being ghoulish about it.'

'She lost a daughter to drowning herself,' I tell her.

'Yes, I heard that after she left, when we all found out who she really was. I expect that's what made her so considerate towards me. Mothers recognize each other's pain.'

'And your son?' I ask. 'Was that how he—'

'Oh no. He returned safely that day, although maybe he'd have been better off lost to the water, considering how his life played out for him afterwards. There are times I think it was a miracle that I held on to him for as long as I did. Sometimes I feel as if God has been punishing me my entire adult life, but, no matter how hard I try, I can't understand what I ever did to offend Him. It's not fair, is it? Life. You'd wonder whether it's all worth the bother.'

She shakes her head sadly, then places a hand atop her son's gravestone, before walking on with a sigh, her head bowed as she makes her way towards the gate that opens on to the laneway and that, in turn, I assume, leads to her lonely home.

The sun is setting.

I make my way down to the beach and watch the waves as they lap towards the shore. Before me is the Atlantic Ocean, sweeping south-east in the direction of Tierra del Fuego, where it will make the bend for the Pacific and travel onwards towards Sydney, Bondi and home.

A sound from behind makes me turn and I watch as Rebecca makes her way towards me. She's barefoot in the sand and I'm glad that she's come alone. Taking her place next to me, we both remain silent for a few moments, staring out towards the horizon.

'I remember when my mother told me she was coming here,' she says eventually without any preamble. 'And how angry I felt. The trial had just ended, of course, and we'd had such a terrible year. I felt she was abandoning me when I needed her most. It's why I punished her. Blocking her number and unblocking it repeatedly. And then, one day, I just showed up out of the blue. She was so surprised to see me.'

'She talked about that,' I reply. 'The night we met for dinner before our wedding.'

'Did she? I don't remember.'

'Yes.'

She turns to me now.

'Thank you,' she says.

'For what?'

'For coming here. For bringing Emmet. It never even crossed my mind that you would do such a thing. When I saw you in the doorway of the pub, I couldn't believe it.'

She reaches out and we take each other's hands, recalling the good times we shared over the years, the laughs, the nights out, the jokes, the hangovers, the work conversations, the tears, the confessions, the traumas, the love.

'I don't want to have the same distance with him as I had with her,' she says, sighing deeply as she turns back towards the waves. 'I need to spend more time with him.'

'You do.'

'I've told myself that I wanted to protect him. From me. From all the anger inside me. But last night, the way he took care of me . . . Furia told me that you told him.'

'You're not angry?'

She shakes her head. 'No,' she says. 'Not at all. If anything, I'm glad you did.'

'I told him about me too.'

'Really?'

'Yes.'

'It was the right time. He'll go back to Australia changed, I suppose, but perhaps in a good way. You've done a good job, Aaron. Better than I ever did. He's lucky to have you. I'm lucky that you're our son's father.'

I feel tears form behind my eyes. It is so peaceful here, just the two of us. It occurs to me that, after Emmet, Rebecca remains the most important person in my life. Someone who I would – quite literally – travel halfway across the world to support.

'I noticed you chatting with Furia,' she says after a moment, smiling.

'Yes, I made a pass, but she was having none of it.'

She laughs.

'You're happy together?'

'We are.'

'I'm glad.'

'Thank you.'

'She gave you what I never could.'

She doesn't reply, but I can tell from her expression that she knows I'm right. I've spent so long lying to

myself about what went wrong between us that it's time
for me to face the truth.

'All those years we spent together,' I say, 'you needed
more than my words. More than my endless romantic
gestures. You needed someone who would touch you.
God, it's not like you didn't tell me often enough.' I take a
deep breath and just say what needs saying. 'You needed
sex. You needed to feel loved in that way.'

She nods.

'I did, Aaron.'

'I've spent years telling myself that it was the other
way around. That it was you who didn't want to touch
me. I've lied to myself, to my therapist. Because I couldn't
face it. I'm that thing that Emmet talks about.'

She frowns. 'What thing?'

'The unreliable narrator.'

'It wasn't your fault, Aaron,' she tells me. 'It was hers.
I won't even say her name.'

'I know. You begged me to seek therapy, and I refused.
I should have listened. I've never allowed myself to truly
believe that I didn't have a part in all of that. To accept
that I was the victim. I've never given myself a chance
to heal. And that wasn't fair on you. Or Emmet. Or our
family.'

'It's not too late,' she tells me, putting an arm around my
shoulder and pulling me close. 'That woman destroyed
a piece of you, and you can't allow her to keep doing so.
She's in prison for the rest of her life, and you're only
forty. You have more than half your life ahead of you, all
going well. Emmet told me that you're still single.'

'I am.'

'That there hasn't been anyone since I left.'

'There hasn't.'

She steps away now and looks me directly in the eye, placing her hands on my arms.

'I'm going to tell you something now, Aaron,' she says. 'And I want you to listen. Because I mean it. Because you're my friend.'

I nod.

'You deserve to be loved.'

When night falls, I find myself back on the beach, alone on the sand. It's dark now. The moon is out. Stars stud the sky. I close my eyes and take a deep breath of the cleanest air that has ever filled my lungs.

Slowly, I take off my clothes and walk naked towards the water, wanting to plunge deep down into the waves. I stay beneath the surface for as long as I can before bursting through the surface, gasping for air. I brush the hair out of my eyes and look back towards the island. I've swum a little further out than I expected but, while I may be a terrible surfer, one of the benefits of living in Sydney all these years is that I've become a strong swimmer. The water is calm too, so I know I'm in no danger. In the distance, smoke is rising from the chimneys of the cottages where fires have been lit.

But I'm not ready to return just yet, so float on my back, looking up at the blackness above me. I think about my conversation with Rebecca from earlier and know how right she was. Freya Petrus stole so much of my life, and I simply can't allow her to lay claim to another minute. I refuse to be her victim any longer; I want to be her survivor. But how?

It's then, out of the night sky, that a voice seems to whisper in my ear. The voice of a woman I met only a few times and whose body is now settling into its eternal coffin, deep in the earth of a church graveyard no more than a couple of miles from here.

Don't go home, Aaron, she tells me.

Not yet, anyway.

Stay here. Stay on the island.

For a few months. Perhaps even a year.

Move into the cottage.

Heal.

Grow strong.

Allow Rebecca and Emmet the space to find each other again while you're away.

And when you're ready, when the time comes, go back to Australia and start over.

And yes, I tell myself. This is exactly what I will do. I'll tell them both in the morning and hope that they'll be happy for me. A year at most. Rebecca can base herself out of Sydney during that time and, when she's away for work, Emmet can stay with Damian's family. They'll be happy to have him.

I must remain on this unlikely rock, this final outpost of human life before the Atlantic Ocean stretches towards America, and prepare for my second life, one that I will embrace when I feel the strength and confidence to do so.

I plunge back down now, blocking out all the noise of the world around me, but keep my eyes open, staring into the dark black depths of the water, feeling the tug of the earth, the fire within me and the air that remains in my lungs.

I'm not there yet, but one day I will be. At one with myself, at one with the universe, and – finally – at one with the elements.

John Boyne is the author of eighteen novels for adults, six for younger readers, a collection of short stories and a picture book. His 2006 novel *The Boy in the Striped Pyjamas* has sold more than eleven million copies worldwide and has been adapted for cinema, theatre, ballet and opera. He has won four Irish Book Awards, including Author of the Year in 2022, along with a host of other international literary prizes. His novels are published in sixty languages, making him the most translated Irish writer of all time.

X (formerly Twitter): @JohnBoyneBooks
Instagram: @JohnBoyneAuthor